This is a work of fiction. Names, characters, places, and events are either the product of the author's imagination or used in a fictitious manner. Any resemblance to actual persons, living or dead, locals or actual events is purely coincidental.
This work is an anthology of Bulwark.

Illustrations by RL Jackson
No part of this publication may be reproduced, transmitted, stored, etc. Without the written permission of the author.
Copyright © 2019 Chelshire, Inc.
All rights reserved.
ISBN-13: 978-1-947188-91-4

Bulwark

BRIT LUNDEN

DEDICATION

For my family

CONTENTS

1

"It's like a primordial soup," Clay Finnes muttered, his hands on his hips.

"A primordial what?" Owen Bishop raised his hangdog face to look at the town sheriff.

"Primordial, ancient, prehistoric . . ." Clay looked at the deputy's blank face and finished with, "old . . . really, really old."

"Oh," Owen shook his craggy head. His bulbous eyes looked like two hard-boiled eggs, and his hair was matted as if glued to the top of his round head. Owen never passed any of the tests allowing him to advance in the force. He was a deputy when Clay first got a job in Bulwark, right out of the army. As the promotions started coming, Clay eventually became his boss. He wondered if it bothered the older man to be taking direction from someone who had trained under him.

"You mean like dinosaurs?" Owen scratched his head. "Dino . . . no . . . forget it, Owen. What else did the couple say?" He listened to Owen drone on about the car that was now sitting in the middle of the greenish pond.

"Appears they were coming from the other side." Owen pointed vaguely in the other direction.

"How could they? There's nothing there. That road's been closed off for years."

Something was wrong. Clay wasn't sure what, but a feeling of unease enveloped him until his body fairly vibrated with it.

Clay looked up, his deep brown eyes scanning the thicket of trees surrounding the strange body of water that seemed to have appeared overnight. He crinkled his nose; the pond smelled pretty bad too. It was a greenish color, like dirty army fatigues. It seemed shallow. He resisted the urge to stick the toe of his boot in the water. It was still, the surface like polished glass. The Ford Fusion was trapped in what appeared to be the deepest part of the puddle, as if the driver had tried to speed through it. Clay estimated the brackish water was about two feet deep.

"If they had skirted the edges, they would have made it through. He shoulda used the choke, probably got an entire engine full of water." Once Owen started talking, he could go on about something forever.

"Where the hell were they coming from?" Clay muttered to himself. He moved away as if to see through the gloom. "It's a road that leads to nowhere."

He took off his hat, wiping his sweaty forehead with the back of his hand. It was hotter than usual. No breeze ruffled the leafy trees or relieved the stifling humidity that made his shirt stick to his back.

There was nothing—no sound, not the buzzing of bees or the droning sound of mosquitoes. Not a bird in sight or the croaking music of frogs in the late afternoon. When he got home, he'd mention it to Jenna—his wandering thoughts came to an abrupt halt. There would be no conversation. Jenna wasn't there anymore. His family's old farmhouse only had one occupant now. His wife had up and left him. Clay's chest tightened, his throat closing up. His entire life changed and would never be the same. Losing Claire was just the beginning of the end. After that had happened, it was as though they were stuck in some nightmare and couldn't get out.

"Well," Owen continued, oblivious to his boss's distracted air. "The car hit the . . . um . . . water, at a high rate of speed, I think. It must've started to sink."

"It's not deep enough to sink," Clay watched his deputy scratch his bald head then turned to look at the enormous puddle. It covered the road from one end to the other.

3

He chewed the inside of his cheek. He had to admit, it appeared larger than when he had arrived. It couldn't be that deep, could it? Clay forced his attention back to Owen. It helped him stop thinking of his own life. "Where are they?"

"Over at JB's house. The wife's pretty freaked out."

"JB?" Clay liked the retired football pro, had shared quite a few stories with the old vet.

"Over what? The puddle?" The interruption came from Dayna Dalton, a reporter from the *Bulwark Advance*. She was walking toward them, a camera hung around her exposed neck, a spiral notebook clasped in her hand. "Think somebody dropped a load of waste here?"

Clay looked at her. His cheek twitched. Her buttons straining, her clothes were so tight, they looked like they had been painted on her body. She shook her mane of red hair like an angry mare. He turned his gaze away, knowing it annoyed her. No matter how much she pranced around in her tight jeans, he wasn't interested. She hadn't done anything for him in high school, and she didn't do anything for him now. Somehow, it never stopped her from trying to get him to notice her. Clay was tired of it. He sighed heavily.

She came around the back of the car, moving into his personal space. For a minute, Clay thought about backing up, but damn it all, he was the sheriff. He stood his ground, daydreaming how Dayna would react if he threw her into the stinky, green lake that had seemingly developed overnight.

Dayna repeated her comment about someone dropping waste. Clay shrugged indifferently then turned to Owen, ignoring her.

He could feel her bristling but refused to move. He dug his feet in the dark soil, his arms folded over his chest. "JB see anything? Maybe notice something out of place?"

Owen shook his head. "Nope. Nada. I asked. Been quiet. JB said this started small. Says he has a few pictures on his laptop he can send us." Owen paused and then said, "Wait, he mentioned they had a wolf problem lately."

Clay looked at Owen sharply. "Wolves, there haven't been—hey!"

He saw Dayna take off, her feet scurrying around a clump of bushes.

"Dayna!" Clay called after the reporter, who was dashing up the incline straight to JB Straton's cabin.

2

JB'S CABIN

JB Straton's residence was an old hunter's cabin that the former football player had turned into a home. It was high on a hill overlooking some of the richest forests this side of Macon. JB sat on his rocker, a great hickory thing his wife had purchased when she decorated it rustic chic. The rocker had outlasted her by five years. She had passed away as quietly as she lived, and JB could swear that rocker moved when he thought of her.

JB's knees were gone. He shuffled painfully across the knotted-pine floor to bring two mugs of tea to the shivering couple sitting on the edge of the overstuffed couch. He had given the woman a change of clothes; hers had been shredded to rags. The victim held a cotton dishtowel to a gash on her forehead. The bleeding had slowed, but JB knew head wounds bled like the devil.

She was white with fright, her face bleached of color. Her skin looked like the blood had been drained. The husband was little better. He was an older man. His clothing was rumpled, his hair standing up in a weird halo around his head, his eyes fixed on the wall. A thin line of drool escaped from the corner of his downturned lips.

"I can't believe . . . oh my goodness . . . I'm not sure—Henry." She turned to her husband, shaking his inert form. "Henry, we have to go back."

Henry mumbled incoherently.

"Relax, ma'am. He's in no condition to leave. The sheriff will be here soon." JB paused to glance out the window. "Yeah, he'll be here any moment now. Never seen you around here before," JB said, as he placed the mugs on the coffee table. He made sure to put them on glass coasters. He was proud of that table, made it himself from a giant oak tree he felled and then turned into various pieces of furniture around the cottage. He shellacked it to a high gloss. JB could see his reflection in its shiny surface from where he was standing.

Henry seemed to collapse against the cushions, his mouth moving soundlessly. The woman cleared her throat. She wrung her hands then looked up at him with large, pleading eyes.

"I laced that tea with my best brandy." When neither moved, JB picked up the cup, wrapping the woman's hands around the warm mug.

The woman opened her mouth to speak, but no sound came out.

"It'll keep. Drink the tea," JB said softly.

She took a tentative sip and closed her eyes, shivering for a brief instant.

"Go ahead, drink. It'll make you feel better."

She took a healthy swallow, then another. Her body seemed to melt into the couch, the rigidness relaxing. "We're from Atlanta."

"That's quite a distance." JB glanced at the husband, who looked as if he had dozed off. His body had slid to the left, falling between a couple of the pillows behind him. JB almost got up, but the reassuring rise and fall of his chest was enough to let him know that the man was probably sleeping.

JB knew they had walked a fair amount to get here. The land wasn't flat but rugged with lots of roots, rocks, and brush. The cabin was isolated, just the way he liked it. He looked at the muddy hems of the old man's trousers, hoping they hadn't stained his wife's couch.

He had called an ambulance. Dolly, the dispatcher, had said it would take at least an hour for it to get there. The sheriff could take them in his squad car, anyway, once he was finished examining the wreck and the puddle that made it skid. "Not many people travel the back roads around here," JB said, breaking the silence in the cabin.

The woman looked nervously at her husband. Her eyes darted around the room. She gasped then stood, the blanket JB had wrapped around her legs falling to the floor. She stepped over it toward the mantel, her finger outstretched and shaking.

"That's her!" she said in a shrill voice. "That's her." Her voice faded. She turned to stare at her husband, her face filled with horror. "Henry, get up. We have to get out of here."

JB stood angrily, grabbing the picture frame from the mantel. "Stop that this instant!"

"Who are you people?" The woman backed away from him. She pointed an accusatory finger at him, "You monsters!"

"This is my wife. She's been dead for five years."

The woman shook her head slowly from side to side.

"She's the witch. She's the witch who took my children."

3

DAYNA DALTON, TROUBLE-MAKER

A knock outside broke the charged silence as JB stared as his guests. He placed the picture carefully back in its place on the mantle and said gruffly, "I'll be right back." He opened the door to see a red-haired woman on the porch. She had her hand on the door as if she would force herself in. JB hadn't been the greatest linebacker in the NFL for nothing. He stood firm and asked, "Do I know you?"

"Dayna Dalton from the—"

"That's enough, Dayna." Clay Finnes's big hands moved her out of the way.

JB nodded a greeting. "Glad you're here, Clay. I think something's not quite right."

"Not now," Clay advised.

The female crash victim shuffled unsteadily into the kitchen, her legs wobbly.

She lurched toward Clay frantically. "Sheriff, my kids! His wife is evil!" she rambled in a high-pitched voice. Clay thought he heard her say the word witch.

JB shrugged helplessly. Clay turned to him and said, "Get her out of here." He nodded to the reporter.

"You can't do that." Dayna stamped her foot in protest. "I have a right to interview the couple." She blocked him, stepping in front of him like an offensive lineman from his old team. JB smiled at her slight form, wondering if she was planning on tackling him. Not that he'd mind.

JB chuckled and shook his head. "I don't have a problem if she comes in. She ain't hard on the eyes."

"There's no story here, Dayna. It was just a regular old accident," Clay said.

"Says who?" Dayna's green eyes narrowed with hostility. "You've been excluding me from anything important since that night at the bar."

"That's enough, Dayna," the sheriff said in a cold voice.

JB perked up. "What happened at the bar?"

Clay tipped back his hat, looking down at her from his superior height. "Nothing happened. Nothing at all. JB, please escort her from the house."

11

Dayna's face reddened, her fist balled in rage. "You're right. Nothing happened."

Clay clamped his jaw tight. Damn straight, nothing had happened. Why couldn't he convince Jenna of that, he wanted to know?

He watched JB usher her out and closed the door in her face. That woman had played a major role in ruining his life.

"The bar, huh? Was she the one?" JB asked in a low voice.

Clay nodded, his throat tight. He didn't have time for this.

The female victim was near to collapsing. Clay helped her over to a chair, where she sank in a stupor. "How long for the ambulance?" he asked JB.

"They said it would be about an hour. It's on the other side of the county."

Clay nodded. "Domestic dispute. Stabbing. Sherri's over there."

JB's lips thinned. "Town should have more than one ambulance."

"Budget," Clay said with a shrug of his shoulders. "I'll take them in my car. Any idea what they're talking about?"

"Not a clue. Remind me to tell you about the wolf I saw this morning," he called out, as Clay loaded them into his squad car.

4

The bright lights of the emergency room burned a hole in Clay's retinas. He narrowed his gritty eyes as he looked at the clock on the green wall. It was going on 3:30 in the morning. Too late, he frowned. Jenna was on call. There was no helping it; they were going to see each other.

He walked through the narrow corridors, boots echoing on the linoleum. He gestured to a couple of sleepy orderlies to bring the nearly unconscious couple from the back seat of his patrol car.

The wife had cried the entire way, alternately pleading and obsessing about some strange place she called the gingerbread house. She described a fantastical residence that bordered on something Hollywood would have dreamed up. Clay knew every building in the area and assured her there was no such place in the county. She insisted her children had been abducted and were being held captive at this strange house.

"Linden Lane," she started repeating like a mantra.

He placated her by promising he'd look for Linden Lane and the house she was describing. Clay knew every road in the district and had never heard of this street. He asked her once if she was sure of the name. She looked at him, her eyes bulging from their sockets and whispered, "Linden Lane is on the other side of hell."

The woman started shouting as they loaded her onto a stretcher. Clay sighed wearily, rubbing the spot between his eyebrows, which throbbed with a life of its own. He looked up when he heard the husband's feeble voice.

"It was on the other side of that green lake we drove through," the man mumbled.

Clay leaned over the gurney. "You mean that puddle where your car is stuck?"

"The gingerbread house is on the other side," the man confirmed, his voice a shivery whisper.

"There's a witch!" the woman was shouting. Restraints were put in place to protect her. She strained against them, her face turning purple.

Clay watched her. She probably hit her head on the dash too hard, he reasoned. Maybe she was nuts before the accident. They weren't from around here. "Well, okay, now," he told her. "I'll ask Siri to find it for me."

Once he found out what was going on with these two, he'd check out the deserted stretch of land on the other side of the noxious, growing puddle where their car was stalled. To the best of his recollection, the only thing on the opposite end of that road was an abandoned paper mill on a road that nobody used.

He waited by the tall counter as a nurse checked them in. His passenger was making no sense at this point. She was wailing like a banshee, and her husband had gone catatonic.

Doctor Peter Kent, the resident physician, walked lazily over to Clay. He smiled, his white teeth as blinding as the bright lights overhead. He rested his muscled arms on the Formica countertop, a quizzical look on his face. Clay wondered where the doctor found the time to work day and night and still manage to look like a male model but refrained from asking.

"Morning, Sheriff," the doctor said. "Something going on?"

Clay didn't like Dr. Kent. He was relatively new to town and had somehow developed a reputation as a real lothario. "Love 'em and leave 'em," he had told Clay over drinks one day. Peter Kent had left a trail of broken-hearted nurses littering the hospital corridors. Clay knew Jenna was the prettiest nurse on staff and, as of now, newly single. He groaned inwardly, wishing he could talk to her, replay that final argument. Jenna chose that moment to stumble from the restroom; her skin drained of color.

Clay took one look at her face and knew she was having a panic attack. It was a new thing that began happening soon after they lost Claire. It took him back to the bad times toward the end of their marriage. He remembered the blinding headaches that had crippled her, followed by the sullen silences. He tried to help. Jenna was inconsolable. Not that he was in such a great place, either. Slowly, as the days became months, Jenna had become distant, until one day they had stopped talking altogether.

Clay's breath hitched in his chest, sorrow coming back in a tidal wave. He missed her. His body ached for her, his muscles reacting as if drawn by a powerful magnet. He wondered if he'd ever get used to this new reality. He touched his chest where his heart felt like a leaden lump.

Clay automatically reached for her, and, to his chagrin and anger, Doctor Kent did as well.

"What's wrong, honey?" Clay allowed his broad chest to outmaneuver the leaner physician. "Are you okay?"

She looked frightened.

His wife, well, technically she was still his wife until the papers were signed, looked up, her blue eyes washed with tears. She held a shaky hand to her head.

Doctor Kent took her wrist possessively, checking her pulse, making Clay's back stiffen as if a flagpole had been rammed up his spine.

"What's wrong?" Clay asked.

Jenna stared at him as if she didn't know him. For a second, Clay felt his heart break again. She shook her head. Clay saw her face become a mask once more.

There was a weird vibe between the three of them. "Do you mind?" Clay looked at the doctor, who opened his mouth to reply, when a shout interrupted him.

"Dr. Kent!" The nurse attending the patients yelled. "You're needed."

"Jenna, are you okay to help out or do you need to lie down?" Dr. Kent tilted his head.

Clay's knuckles turned white as he fought the urge to push the doctor away. The skin tightened over his scalp at the familiar tone the doctor used with his wife.

Kent moved toward the curtained cubicles where the new patients had been delivered. Jenna followed him.

Clay reached out for her arm. "What happened? You're not thinking about Claire?"

Jenna shook her head. "No. I have to go."

"I'd like to talk." Clay's eyes bored into hers.

"This is not the time or place. Besides, the time for talking is done, Clay. I can't do it anymore." She eased out of his grip and headed toward the patient area.

Pulling the curtain back, Dr. Kent entered the trauma bay. "Jenna, I need you now! What are the vitals, Mary?"

"I just finished John Doe." She gestured toward the male patient Clay had brought in. "BP is 200 over 110. Respirations are 24. Pulse is 96, and he's satting at 88 percent. The sheriff said the couple was involved in a vehicular accident. EMS was too far off, so the sheriff brought them in."

"Line him up with the X-ray. Get a head and neck CT and pull a metabolic panel. Also get me tox and drug screens, stat. Do we know who was driving?"

"Don't think so," Mary replied. She finished getting the vitals on their second patient as the doctor ordered the same set of tests for the patient referred to as Jane Doe. Dr. Kent began the process of clearing Jane Doe's neck and spine.

Clay watched the doctor's procedures, knowing they were vital. The patients were acting strangely and mumbling incoherently. Dr. Kent was following hospital protocol.

Clay moved closer to observe the ER team working on the two patients. The doctor threw him a look. Clay's eyes narrowed as he stared him down. He smirked when he saw the doctor's jaw muscles clench with fury.

They likely had concussions, Clay thought. Jenna said the same thing out loud. He looked up at her, and their eyes held each other's for a long minute. He couldn't look away, even if he wanted to. Jenna appeared all efficient and calm now. He propped himself against the counter, watching as she moved competently around the room.

The trauma bay was alive with emergencies. The whir of stretchers and wheelchairs being pushed down the halls, the cries of children and adults, and the beeping of monitors and IV pumps all contributed to the organized chaos.

"Full moon," Mary, the other nurse, commiserated.

"Gonna be a busy night." Jenna wrapped heated blankets around Jane Doe's blue-tinged limbs.

"Yes," Clay muttered. "those full moons bring out all the loonies."

"Shhhh." Jenna crossed her eyes and stuck out her tongue at him, playfully. With that face, Jenna's sense of humor resurfaced, bringing in him a longing for the old days when they were best friends and she could make him laugh. For a minute, it felt as if the last year hadn't happened and they were Clay and Jenna again. His body yearned for hers, and he wished his surroundings would fade away and they could just touch each other again, feel that all-encompassing love between them.

The shrill scream of an alarm jolted Clay into reality. With regret, he realized his life had changed and was never going to be the same again. He missed both Jenna and Claire with every fiber of his being. His wife smiled at him, lighting up the drab room. It was a lopsided grin. The tiny dimple he adored appeared, and he longed to kiss her right there. He blushed at the memory and felt a little bit stupid.

"Things are always a little crazier on nights like this," Mary said from across the room, where she was applying pressure to a bloody nose on a drunk college student.

Clay watched them work; it was almost like a ballet. They moved in tandem without communicating. He remembered the night he met Jenna. Gunshot wound to his shoulder. It had started with a traffic stop and escalated to a car chase through half the county, ending in a bloody battle.

It had been a full moon as well. Jenna was the nurse on duty, all crisp efficiency. He made it his mission to melt her icy exterior. It took some time to get her to go for dinner. He swore he'd get shot in the other shoulder if she kept refusing. Finally, she surrendered to his persistent courtship, and there was no going back for either of them. They had a perfect life. They inherited his parent's farmhouse and had a baby—but when tragedy struck, their lives spiraled out of control.

Clay looked up, locking eyes with her, and knew she was thinking about the same thing. His insides turned to mush, and he resisted the urge to grab her and drag her out of there. Sadness weighed him down. He hated his new reality. It wasn't supposed to be like this. They had lived a fairy-tale existence, he, Jenna, and Claire. At least it had been a fairy tale until it turned into a nightmare.

"We've got to run some tests on them. You should leave," Dr. Kent spoke from behind the counter. He was holding an X-ray up to the lighted panel behind him.

"I have questions."

"They are hardly in a condition for an interrogation," Dr. Kent said.

Clay turned away to watch all the activity, seemingly lost in thought. At that moment, Dayna Dalton entered the external door with windblown hair.

"Sheriff Finnes," she called out. When he ignored her, she tried again. "Clay, I have some questions."

Dr. Kent looked up, a smirk on his face.

"Not now, Dayna," Clay said. He looked at Jenna, who was studiously avoiding his eyes. Once Dayna had entered the room, the atmosphere had become chillier.

"Why? Do you have any more information on the witch?" Dayna demanded.

Both Mary and Jenna looked up from where they were working. Jenna glanced at Clay, her eyes wide.

"She was ranting, Dayna. Hardly in her right mind."

"Is that your official statement?"

Clay took the reporter by the arm and escorted her out of the emergency room. Dayna pulled her elbow away, turning to face him. "Let's go to the cafe to talk," she said softly. "I'm sorry, I thought you and Jenna were . . . well, done."

Clay's face hardened. "For a woman who values the truth in her reporting, I find it ironic you live through lying."

"I didn't lie," she spat. "I can't help it. You kissed me. It wasn't the other way around."

"I didn't kiss you—oh, what's the use." He turned, leaving her alone outside and went back into the triage center. That woman was delusional. Clay fumed at his weakness.

Dayna had come onto him right after Jenna told him she needed space—and that they should separate for a bit. It was not a good time for him, and that night Clay had

had one drink too many, but he hadn't kissed her. Clay squashed the feelings of guilt that made him feel angry at himself. He had almost kissed her, but he hadn't. The problem was, Jenna had come after him at the bar that night. Maybe she was having second thoughts. He would never know. Once Jenna had seen Dayna wrapped around him like a boa constrictor, she had moved out of the farmhouse. The look on her face was imprinted in his memory forever.

Mary had left to call the X-ray and the lab. Jenna stayed to hook up the patients' heart monitor and oxygen and start the IVs. Jenna looked up when he walked in, her eyes appearing bruised. She reached for the woman's hand and swabbed it with antiseptic. She took the catheter and began to insert it as the woman gasped.

Clay could hear the woman babbling from across the room. He hurried over.

"The witch, you have to find my children. Look for the gingerbread house!" she sputtered, then choked. She grabbed Jenna's hand in a vice-like grip. "Tell them . . . tell them to look for Linden Lane," she mumbled the words. Her eyes rolled backward in their sockets, and the pupils fixated. Jenna gasped.

The cardiac rhythm abruptly changed as the woman flatlined, setting off an alarm audible to anyone within earshot. Jenna rushed into action. She shoved Clay away from the bed. Calling the code, she opened up the crash cart and got to work, desperate to save the patient.

Clay shouted, "What happened?" Nobody answered.

The team of doctors and nurses surrounded the woman and worked on her for a good ten minutes. Clay watched Dr. Kent throw up his hands. It was over. She was dead.

Jenna shook her head. "I'm calling it." She glanced up at the clock on the wall. "5:15 A.M."

"What was wrong with her?" Clay asked.

"Not sure." Dr. Kent ripped off his gloves. "I'm not sure."

Clay moved to the corner and observed the husband. John Doe was still out of it, in critical but stable condition. A nurse came in and was told to move the bed from the room.

"Where are they taking him?" Clay asked Jenna.

"ICU." She disappeared into another room and didn't come out. Clay rolled his shoulders off the counter and left the hospital.

5

TRAPPED IN BULWARK

Clay slid into his squad car, feeling slightly uneasy. This was torture. Maybe he should take up that new job offer and make a move to Nevada. Owen would finally get a promotion. An old army buddy had told him about an opening in a small town near Vegas. That would put two time zones between him and Bulwark—Three hours and two thousand miles away from Jenna. A new life where he could start over because he couldn't begin anything knowing she was nearby. "Damn it!" He smacked the steering wheel with the flat of his hand. He looked at his stinging palm. Jenna was as much a part of him as his limbs or his heart. He could no sooner leave her than cut himself in half. He was trapped. Trapped in Bulwark.

Time to go to work and stop being maudlin, he reprimanded himself. "Linden, Linden Lane," he whispered, pulling his lip.

Closing his eyes, he tried to picture where it was but came up with nothing. He'd spent almost his entire life in Bulwark, combing every street with his buddies before he left for the army. He couldn't remember a Linden Lane.

With a resigned sigh, he picked up his cell and asked Siri, "Where is Linden Lane in Bulwark?" Siri informed him where Layton Lane was located.

"No, Linden," he insisted.

It took a minute, and Siri responded, "Unable to find Linden Lane in Bulwark, shall I search the web for that for you?"

"Huh." Clay picked up his radio and called the base. He didn't have time for this. "Dolly, you there?"

"Yes, I am, Sheriff. How'd that couple do?" Dolly was old enough to be his grandmother. She chain-smoked and drank bourbon by the bottle. Her voice was as deep as a man's, and her face as leathery as a baseball mitt.

"Not good, Doll. Not good at all."

"Shame."

He heard her click her tongue. "What happened with the stabbing?"

"Damndest thing, Sheriff. The perp stabbed her with a two-pronged fork."

"Domestic fight?"

"Appears so. Stuck her right in the neck like a vampire." Dolly gave a wheezy laugh. "Whole county's falling apart. We've been getting a mess of calls on wolf sightings."

"Well, we both know that's as impossible as a vampire biting someone in a trailer park."

Dolly was silent for a minute then said in a wounded voice, "I don't invent the calls, Sheriff. Sometimes the truth is stranger than fiction," she added cryptically.

Clay rolled his eyes. The old girl was touchy tonight.

"I didn't call your integrity into question, Dolly. Red wolves are virtually extinct 'round here. Must be a pack of wild dogs on the loose."

"Okay . . . wolves or dogs, what do you want me to do about it?"

"Where?" he asked.

"That's the interesting thing." He heard her take a long drag on her cigarette.

"You're not smoking, Dolly, are you? You know it's not allowed in the office anymore." He waited for her to answer. "Dolly?"

"Stupid rules," she grumbled.

"Did Owen bring you a sample of the green water?" Clay changed the subject.

"Yes, I presume you want me to send it to Atlanta for analysis? Just want to remind you with the state shut down, it's gonna take a few weeks to get answers."

"Sheesh. Damn government budget and their bullshit." Clay paused for a second. "Now tell Owen to check out the wolves." He looked at his wristwatch. "Sherri's left for the day?"

"Yup." Dolly was not a talkative person, which could be useful sometimes and a pain in the ass at others.

"Okay. Tell Owen to take Terence with him." Terence was the rookie. He was a fresh-faced kid from the neighborhood who had hung around the office his entire life. He had finally joined the force this year.

"Dolly?" Clay said impatiently.

"I sent that boy home hours ago. He didn't look so good."

Clay pressed the button on the radio. "Stop babying him. He's been sworn in. He's old enough to serve and protect." Clay sighed heavily. "Dolly, you ever hear of a street called Linden Lane?" If anyone knew the back roads of Bulwark, it was old Dolly Summars.

Clay waited while she searched her memory. Took her own sweet time, he thought.

"Doll, you there?"

"Who told you about Linden Lane?" Her voice quivered a bit. "You don't need to go to Linden Lane. Forget you ever heard about it." This came out in a rush, sounding angry.

"What's the matter with Linden Lane?"

There was silence. Clay clicked the button, the last shreds of his patience evaporating.

"Dolly! Get me the directions. Now," he growled.

"It's on the east side of town." Dolly's voice was quiet as if she was reluctant to tell him. "You know where the old mill is?"

"Where they closed the road? Nobody lives down there. No access," Clay said.

He heard Dolly huff through the radio. "Not no more, they don't. Used to. Used to be a family there. Not there no more since the mill closed. Just forget about it. Forget you heard of Linden Lane."

Clay thought about the ruins of the paper mill. It had been closed for over twenty years. Sometimes vagrants crashed there. It was on the other side of that puddle. "Yeah. Go on."

"Behind the mill is a street, it's little more than a dirt path. That's where Linden Lane can be found." There was a pause. "Clay . . . If you're gonna go—"

"Yes?"

"Take Owen with you."

"Nope, send him on the wolf . . . I mean the dog calls." As if on cue, a wolf cried in the hills, followed by another. That was weird. Clay knew the call of a wolf, and those were definitely of the lupine variety. A shiver raced up his spine. He shook it off. He scratched his head, thinking maybe they had traveled up from Florida or escaped from a circus. Did a circus even have wolf acts?

He stood outside of the car, searching the darkness for something, anything, the continuing calls causing his skin to prickle on his scalp.

"Tell Owen to get on it now!" He threw the receiver on the seat and sat back down in his cruiser. The halogen lights painted the emergency entrance orange. The hospital's automatic doors whooshed open. Jenna walked out and leaned against the brick of the building. Their eyes met, and she rested her head against the building as if she carried the weight of the world. Clay fought the impulse to go to her and peeled off into the night.

6

GINGERBREAD HOUSE

Light crept over the treetops, chasing the shadows away. Clay rubbed his tired eyes. They burned with fatigue.

He saw JB's cabin through the shrubs, the windows dark, not even the television flickering. The old guy must be tired from all the action.

Clay skirted the puddle, driving on the shoulder of the road. He heard the water hit the outside of the car, watching it ripple behind him as he proceeded through slowly. He paused, trying to remember how far the mill was, then drove in the direction of the ruins.

Scrubby pines surrounded the buildings. The concrete was broken in several places, with weeds filling in the gaps. It was early in the morning now, that time when the air is wet with dew and the silence fails to comfort. It felt as if the forest was holding its breath, waiting for something to happen.

Clay searched the massive compound, his practiced eyes looking for movement. The mill used to provide hundreds of jobs but had closed down sometime when he was a kid, maybe twenty years ago. It was now as silent as a tomb.

He slowed the car, looking for a street until he was well past the buildings. Nothing. He turned the vehicle, circling back, moving at a snail's pace and looking for the entrance to Linden Lane.

He threw the car into park, got out, and walked the perimeter of the property. The wind picked up, scattering leaves and other debris around the abandoned building. A gate swung, the screeching metal electrifyingly loud in the silence. Clay narrowed his eyes, spying a rutted path. He walked over, crouching, touching the red soil. The road was smoother here. Using his hand, he wiped the surface of the road, his fingers turning rusty as he scraped away layers of dirt. The patch turned black, as an asphalt road was revealed. "Bingo."

Clay stood, brushing his palms together. They looked stained red, as if with blood. The soil always startled him with the intensity of its color. It was as if it held the inhabitants' lifeblood, collected from its violent past. Bulwark had seen its share of drama over the years; it had been the site of a major Civil War battle. Of course, there were natural disasters like hurricanes and tornados. Bulwark was a hotbed during the civil rights movement and there were always tales of hauntings in the old plantation houses. He peered down the road into the gloomy distance, a thick layer of fog obscuring his view. He turned to go back to his cruiser when a sound stopped him in his tracks.

He heard laughter, children's laughter. It was faint at first, growing in volume until it felt as if it filled his head. He looked around, seeing nothing but the desolate mill, a dirt road, and the dense foliage. He got into his car and proceeded down the dirt lane.

He rode for what seemed an hour. Raggedy brush bordered the road; his windshield was dusted red, as if it had been bathed in blood rather than soil. He had driven in a snowstorm once in the mountains. He remembered thinking it felt like he was in a rocket ship, the snow looking like stars as he drove. If that memory was like flying in space, being here on Linden Lane was like being on Mars. The rich, red Georgia clay coated the car crimson. Clay stepped lightly on the gas, driving cautiously as the mists grew thicker. He could barely see a foot in front of him. He wondered where the sun had gone. It was supposed to be hot and humid; the morning sun should have burned off the fog.

BULWARK

Clay slowed the car and finally stopped in front of a postal box. He got out, his feet crunching on gravel, knowing he was at his destination. Vines covered the old tin mailbox, the faded lettering barely discernible. His fingers brushed the leaves from the rusty metal. It read Bavmorda. He peered at the name: Bavmorda Gingerbread House, Linden Lane.

The drive was a rutted mess; trees reached out to meet in the middle of the path. Clay brushed away the vines, feeling them cling to his arms. He ripped them off impatiently. The house was a faded white Victorian, the paint chipped and worn. The eaves were high, the uneven roofline dripping with fretwork. He knew they called these design elements gingerbread. Jenna liked that sort of thing. He thought it was creepy.

The door was black, a dull brass knocker in the center, a fan window covered with a greasy film of dust at the top.

He heard a clatter from above, but the hulking form of the house blotted out the skyline. He stepped up the warped steps, the wood creaking noisily. Raising the knocker, he banged against the door, waiting for a response. He called out, "Sheriff. Open up."

It felt like he waited forever. He stood straighter when the black door creaked open, revealing a shriveled old woman, her white hair lank around her wrinkled face. The smell was horrific. It seeped through the doorway like a noxious gas.

Clay recoiled from the stench as she opened the door, the smell overwhelming him. He had arrested a hoarder once. The woman had lived with over a hundred cats, many of them dead. The house was a biohazard. This house had that same odor.

"What do you want?" the woman asked in a quivery voice.

Clay tried to get a good look at her, but her tangled hair obscured her face. She seemed familiar, but he couldn't place her. Memories of his fourth-grade teacher teased him. He shivered involuntarily.

The woman blurted, "This is private property." She began to close the door.

Clay propped his foot in the doorjamb, preventing her from slamming the door. "I'd like to have a word with you," he informed her. "I don't recall ever seeing this house before."

She stayed on her side of the door, her gnarled hands squeezing the wood. "My family's been here for generations, Sheriff. What do you want?" she asked rudely.

Clay wracked his brain. He couldn't think of anyone named Bavmorda. "How long have you lived here?" he asked.

"Years. As far as I know, that is not a crime, Sheriff. Is that all?" She moved her face so that it came into the light. Her eyes looked like black holes in her wizened skull. For a minute, he thought he was looking at a corpse.

She opened her mouth, revealing gray teeth. Her breath stank. Clay fought the urge to gag; the smell was overpowering.

Clay recoiled, backing away from the door, the heavy weight of the odor squeezing the breath from his body.

She was just an old woman, one part of his brain assured him. The other half told him to get the hell out of there.

She laughed loudly, her voice a cruel cackle. There was a thud. A roof tile landed at Clay's feet. Both their gazes moved to the shingle. It had a crescent-shaped, round bite mark. Clay bent to pick it up.

"I wouldn't if I were you," she cautioned.

He looked at her then picked it up to study it. He heard a sound above him, like footsteps, as if someone were running on the roof.

"Kids will be kids." She laughed and slammed the door.

"Kids?" he repeated, looking upward. He saw the outline of a person, a small figure. "Hey," he called out. He watched the figure skitter out of sight.

Clay backed away, trying to look at the roof. The sun was out. He shaded his eyes but saw nothing beyond the bright, blue morning.

He left for town, knowing he'd be back. There was something familiar about that woman's face. The accident victim had it all wrong; she looked nothing like JB's dead wife. She looked like his fourth-grade teacher, the meanest woman in the school. What the hell was her name? He couldn't remember, but he knew for sure it wasn't Bavmorda.

7

BOBBY RAY, TROUT, AND A
BURLAP BAG

Clay drove back toward the Old Mill, his thoughts on the elderly woman he met at the gingerbread house. Certainly, he understood why the accident victim had thought she was a witch. She was crooked and frail, with an enormous nose. Clay saw the curtains twitch. He felt her cold eyes watching him as he left her driveway.

He looked in his rearview mirror; a mist appeared, obscuring the house as if it had never existed. A shiver raced up his spine, and he shuddered. He pressed his foot on the gas, picking up speed. He wanted to get out of there.

Soon, he arrived at the puddle, and damn if it didn't look bigger. He searched the surrounding area looking for a broken pipe or something creating the mess. The smell was worse, a cross between a skunk and rotten eggs. He was happy when he put the quagmire behind him.

Movement caught his eye: the leaves rippled. A large burlap bag was ejected from the bushes. It lay writhing on the road, as if it were packed with a bunch of snakes. It was big enough to hold Dolly, Clay thought inanely. Clay slammed on the brakes, jumping from the car, his gun unholstered. "Come out with your hands up!"

He heard a curse and the sound of someone dropping something.

"I said, 'hands up!'"

The footsteps moved clumsily toward the clearing. Clay saw two sets of worn boots. "Come out slowly," he ordered. Lowering his gun, he shook his head as Bobby Ray and his half-wit cousin, Trout, exited from the overgrowth.

"What are you two up to?" he asked, putting away his gun. "If you're killing kittens again, we are going to have a problem." He peered at the wiggling bag; it stopped moving.

Bobby Ray looked up at him, his dark eyes filled with hatred. "Don't be talking to me like I'm some kind of criminal, Clayton Finnes. Ain't no crime in camping."

Trout shifted from foot to foot.

"You nervous about something, Trout?"

"No, Suh."

"Don't be callin' him suh, Trout," Bobby Ray spat. "He ain't older 'n us. He jus' got a badge that makes him think he's special."

"That so, Bobby Ray?" Clay asked. He didn't like the Parkers. They were a crazy bunch, and he had a history with Bobby Ray that stretched back to grade school.

Bobby Ray was a bully. Jenna didn't like him either. Bobby Ray was his first collar in law enforcement. He had got him on a robbery charge. Bobby Ray went away for a year and a half. When he was released, Clay had found him outside Jenna's house. He and Jenna had just started dating. He took Bobby Ray in again on a trespassing charge back then. It had caused more bad blood than transfusion could fix.

Clay gestured to the burlap. "What's in the bag?"

"Rabbits," Trout said. Bobby Ray elbowed him in the ribs.

"Snakes."

Clay eyed the moving bag and laughed. "Well, which is it, rabbits or snakes?"

Trout looked at Bobby Ray and said, "Both."

Clay turned thoughtful for a minute. "Either of you knows a lady by the name of Bavmorda? Lives over in a place called the gingerbread house?"

Bobby Ray motioned with his arms, as if asking permission to lower them. Clay nodded.

"No," Bobby Ray stammered; his face looked odd. He went all green and sickly looking. "Ain't nobody living on that side of town."

"Something wrong with you?" Clay peered closer into the gloom. A fog rolled in with a layering mist that coated everything with a wet film of water. Mosquitoes droned, and, in the distance, a wolf howled.

Both cousins looked around nervously. "Is that a wolf?"

Clay laughed. "There are no wolves around here, Bobby Ray. You know that. It's got to be a coyote." Clay moved toward the wiggling bag on the ground when the greenish head of a cottonmouth poked out. The sheriff jumped backward.

"Woah! What are you collecting cottonmouth's for?"

Trout said "We like 'em. We like the skins." He pointed toward the empty bag and whined, "You done lost us our snake, Sheriff."

Clay made a sound of disgust. He pivoted to walk to his car. Pausing for a second, he turned around. Bobby Ray and his cousin Trout were gone. The only thing left was a puddle of blood where the snake- or rabbit-filled bag had rested.

He watched the stain on the road in his rearview mirror as he pulled out heading back to town. He didn't get far when his radio squawked. Dolly's voice sounded urgent.

"Sheriff. You there?"

"Yeah, Dolly. What's the matter?"

"Head over to the Holsteam farm. There's been a possible murder."

"Sheesh," Clay sighed. His peaceful little town was becoming a crime scene. "Who's the victim?"

The radio was silent for so long, Clay asked again, then warned, "Dolly, I have one nerve left, and you're doing the polka on it."

"Owen. Deputy Owen Bishop's been torn apart by your nonexistent wolves."

Clay put on his siren and lights as he tore down the road toward the furthest edge of the county. Sam Holsteam stood outside, his face pasty, his finger pointing to a lump in the middle of his yard.

A tarp had been thrown over the body, but blood leaked sluggishly down the damp, red earth. Around them the peach trees gave off their perfume, the wind rustling their leaves.

"What happened?"

"I tol' him to wait for backup. He didn't listen. Owen Bishop was never the brightest bulb in the marquee."

Clay looked up, his face wooden.

"With all due respect, I liked the guy, but he could be a real blockhead sometimes," Sam rambled.

"Get to the story, Sam." Clay got down on one knee and lifted the tarp. He gagged. Owen was a mess; his throat had been ripped out. "Any idea who did this?"

"Not who, but what. Was a werewolf."

Clay stood wearily. "You drinking that peach moonshine, again, Sam? I swear, this time I'm busting you."

Sam backed away, his hands in front of him. "I didn't touch a drop. Full moon last night. I heard that beast howling. Stole at least a dozen of my chickens. I thought it was those Parker boys, you know, Trout and Bobby Ray?"

Clay shook his head. "Couldn't be; I just saw them. They were on the other side of town." His cell vibrated in his pocket. He ignored it.

"It weren't them," Sam agreed. "I saw it. It was a wolf with silver fur. It was as tall as me and as wide as my barn door."

"Oh, come on . . . ."

"How else do you explain what happened to Owen?" The ambulance pulled up, followed by a squad car. Terence hopped out of the patrol car. Sherri was driving the ambulance.

"I thought Dolly sent you home," Clay said to Terence. He was young and inexperienced, the newest member of the force.

"Been listening to my scanner. I thought you'd need me." Terence held up a camera to record the evidence.

"Busy night?" Sherri asked as she walked toward them. Sherri was ex-army, just like him. She had gingery hair pulled into a ponytail that she should have stopped wearing ten years ago. She was tough and could outdrink him any day of the week. Sherri was pulling on blue disposable gloves to handle the body. She lifted the covering, then gasped in shock. "Oh my God!" She dropped the tarp, running to the bushes to empty her stomach.

Clay's radio chirped, his phone rang at the same time.

He answered his two-way.

"Clay?"

"What now, Dolly?"

"You have to head over to Timber Lane."

Clay's gut tightened into a knot. "Which house?"

"Fourteen. There's been a break-in."

Clay pulled out his cell phone. He had two missed calls. Both were from Jenna. She was calling from her new house, Fourteen Timber Lane.

8

A BREAK-IN

"Go," Sherri told him. "I'll take care of this." She shook her head. "It's not like any of us can help Owen anyway."

Clay nodded and got into his cruiser. His body screamed with fatigue, but all he could think about was Jenna. He tore up the distance and made it there in record time.

Jenna's Volkswagen was parked in the designated spot in front of the condo. He pulled in next to it, ran up the steps, and rapped impatiently on the door. Jenna opened it, her face wet with tears, her eyes wide with fright. "Clay," she said with relief.

Without thinking, he reached forward, taking her in his arms. She fit naturally in the spot next to his heart. He rested his chin on top of her head. Clay wanted this moment to last forever. He heard someone clear their throat noisily. Peter Kent stood in the hallway, as if he belonged there.

Clay felt his body tense, and his hands balled into fists.

Jenna pulled away, her face turning pink. "You didn't answer my calls." She wouldn't meet his eyes. "I called Mary, and Peter heard what happened."

"Yes, I came as fast as I could," the doctor said.

"Well, thanks, Dr. Kent. I can handle it from here." The two men stood looking at each other like it was a gunfight.

Jenna handed a jacket to the doctor. "Thanks, Pete. I'm okay. I was just a little nervous," she said with a hint of apology in her voice.

Dr. Kent swaggered passed Clay, a smirk on his face. He stopped at the door and looked at Jenna. Clay reached backward and slammed the door behind him.

"Nothing is going on between us," Jenna said. "Not that it matters, anyway. In a few weeks we won't even be married." Her voice trailed off.

Clay knew she could see the muscles of his jaw working. He brushed past her into the living room. It looked like a motel room; there were no touches of Jenna in the house, not a pillow or a picture. He went to the double doors to a small patio. The lock was broken.

"Any idea who did this?" he asked.

Jenna shook her head, twin tears leaking from her eyes.

"What? It's not that bad. I don't see much damage. Probably kids." He glanced around the room with a practiced eye. The television was intact. There were no signs of anything being taken. "Doesn't look like they stole anything."

She sobbed loudly, rushing into his arms again. "They took Claire's things."

"What?" He held her at arm's length. "What kind of twisted person would do a thing like that?" He studied her face then caressed it with the palm of his hand.

Jenna looked up at him, hope blooming on her tear-stained face. "Do you think this means she could be alive?"

Clay's lips tightened. Jenna said, "Do you need a drink? I've got some bourbon."

Clay shook his head and replied, "Can't. I'm on duty."

Jenna clutched his hand and dragged him toward the kitchen. "Stay, I'll make coffee."

Clay sat at the table holding a mug between his cold hands. He knew he should leave, but he couldn't. Jenna was nervous. She paced a bit then asked if he would stay while she showered. He nodded curtly, and she skittered out of the kitchen. He looked at the poor excuse that served as a lock on her door and shook his head.

"Why don't you have an alarm yet?" he shouted to her in the other room.

He heard her moving around; a door closed, a drawer squeaked. "I don't know. I can't see this place as permanent."

Clay looked at the bare walls, silently agreeing with her. He closed his eyes; the image of Owen's brutalized body scarred on his brain. "Well, either way," Clay swallowed, clearing his throat. "Get one installed as soon as possible. Call Hank. You need the number?"

He heard her murmur a response and knew she would forget the moment he left. He texted a message to Hank, asking for him to stop by and install an alarm later today.

He was used to taking care of her. It came naturally.

He thought about Claire, his gut tightening. He bit his lip, angry and frustrated. What kind of sicko would do something like this? One year ago this week, Claire had been taken from her room in the middle of the night. The kidnapping had just about killed Jenna. She had had a breakdown and ended up in a hospital for a couple of months. He had worked himself sick as well, but some people wear their wounds on the inside. He got up to refill his cup. He heard the bathroom door open, and Jenna stuck her head out of the room. Her blonde hair was wrapped in a towel, and her skin was shiny from the scrubbing.

"Hungry?" he asked, falling into a familiar routine. "I'll make some eggs," he told her, feeling as though they were back in the old days again.

She smiled and disappeared. Clay searched the cabinets, found a bowl, and scrambled a half-dozen eggs. Bending, he located a frying pan, put a knob of butter in it, and rooted through the fridge for something to throw in the omelet. He paused; it felt like nothing had ever happened to them, as if they were back in the early days before the breakdown, before Jenna had thought he had betrayed her, and before they had lost Claire.

She came out wearing yoga pants and a tee he didn't recognize. He placed the eggs between them on the table. Jenna poured more coffee and sat cross-legged in her chair. It was awkward for a second. Jenna and Clay both reached for the serving spoon, their fingers touching. Clay closed his eyes and felt a tingle straight to his heart. When he opened them, he saw that Jenna was smiling shyly. They clasped their hands for a moment and time hung heavy. Jenna laughed nervously and withdrew her hand. Clay took her plate and filled it with food. "You've lost too much weight."

Jenna gave a half-shrug. "Not that hungry."

"You should eat more," Clay growled, loading up her plate. He motioned for her to eat, and she took a forkful of eggs.

"Yum. I always said you were a master in the kitchen."

Clay couldn't resist responding. "Times were you thought I was pretty good in some of the other rooms."

Jenna blushed. He stared at her, at the soft angles of her face, the place where her pulse beat near the dewy skin of her neck. Clay wanted to reach out and take her hand, but pride held him in place. He didn't know what had happened, how his marriage had imploded the way it did. Claire had been taken, Jenna had had her breakdown, his grief took him to the town watering hole where . . . well, none of that mattered. Jenna thought he had betrayed her, and somehow the fight had escalated until they both stood staring at each other, knowing there was no going back. Clay's jaw tightened. Why didn't he take her in his arms and kiss her distrust and anger away? He didn't do it as their marriage disintegrated. He didn't do it now. His arms were frozen, and he didn't understand. He had stormed out with anger and too much pride. What was said couldn't be unsaid.

"You look tired." She smiled at him sympathetically, pulling him from his dark thoughts. "You can crash here . . . on the couch if you want to."

50

The air stilled around them, sound receded, and a vestige of their intimacy returned. Clay felt his heart beat faster with hope. Their eyes locked. He opened his mouth to answer, but his radio chirped, causing them both to jump in their seats.

"Duty calls."

"It always does." She shrugged. That had been an issue too. Somehow, he'd forgotten that. Jenna had felt he worked too hard, that he hadn't spent enough time with her and Claire. He explained that he loved his job and wanted to protect her and the baby—a fat lot of good that did.

He got up with a sigh. He wanted to grab Jenna and kiss her into oblivion. The radio made its presence known again. He wasn't going to let the opportunity go. Not again. He leaned over, their lips almost touching. She pulled away, but he saw her eyes soften. He moved forward, grazing her mouth, their gazes meeting. They stood staring at each other for an endless minute. She moistened her lips with the tip of her tongue. Clay groaned, grabbing her by the shoulders and lifting her against his body. He wrapped her in his embrace, his mouth slanting over hers, her body going boneless against him. Their foreheads touched. He was breathing heavily.

"I . . . are you coming back?" she asked, her voice a whisper.

Clay smiled, his heart filling with hope. "Lock the doors." He felt energized. Despite his extreme exhaustion and the fact that the town was falling around him, Jenna had kissed him back.

9

AUTOPSY

Clay pulled into the sheriff's office parking lot by 9:30 a.m. He knew he needed to sleep, but Owen's death weighed heavily on his mind. He walked a half block to the undertaker, where Doc Swenson would be doing a post-mortem.

Just as he expected, the doc was examining Owen's corpse. The room smelled of formaldehyde, an odor that never failed to clog his nostrils. He heard a door slam but couldn't take his eyes off the collection of organs on the scale beside the doctor.

The physician looked up as he walked into the room. "You look like shit. When was the last time you slept?" His face mask muffled his voice.

"Been a while. Too much to do. I'm down a set of hands." Clay pointed to Owen's body.

"You make up with Jenna, yet?" the doctor asked baldly. Clay opened his mouth to tell him to shut up but snapped it closed. Doc Swenson had delivered both him and Jenna as infants. He guessed the doctor had the right to ask a question like that.

"You know I haven't. She won't talk about it."

"Seems to me that talking is not the right move. Go home and take your wife in your arms—"

"That's enough, Doc. It is what it is." Clay gestured to another table where a corpse lay draped in a white sheet. "That the domestic violence case?"

The doctor nodded.

"Oh, Clay. Never thought I'd see something like this again."

"Pardon?"

Doctor Swenson wiped his bloody hands on the disposable gown. He pulled down the mask and shook his head. "Sad day in Bulwark. Owen Bishop was a good man."

"What did you say about seeing something like this again?"

The doctor waved his hand dismissively. "Been years. Maybe fifty or more. There was a rash of this type of thing." He gestured to the bodies. "I was just out of medical school."

"What exactly are you talking about?" Clay followed the doctor to the outer room where he sat down slowly on a metal chair.

The doctor sighed. "Throats ripped out. Usually, the victims were vagrants. There was a cluster of them. We thought it was a pack of wild dogs."

"You're not going to talk about the wolf nonsense, are you? I never saw anything about it in the records."

"You won't either. It was in the days before computers." The doctor walked to a sink where he ripped off his gloves and washed his hands. "Besides, we all decided it was best forgotten."

"Best forgotten? You sound like an old movie." Clay shook his head.

"Still, it's in the past." The doctor's voice sounded far away, laced with regret.

"It can't be related," Clay said, then added. "Besides, the other guy died from a puncture wound inflicted by his wife."

The doctor's eyebrows rose to the highest point on his forehead. "Nary a drop of blood in his body."

"He bled out?"

"Bone dry."

Clay got up and walked back to the corpse. He raised the sheet to stare at the chalky skin. Twin holes were in the victim's neck.

"He couldn't have bled to death from these."

The doctor agreed with a nod then opened a drawer, taking out a silver flask. He offered Clay a drink. Clay shook his head. The doctor took a long draught. "Look at this."

He held out his hand. In the palm was a bloody tooth, ripped out of a mouth, the root still attached. It had to be two-and-a-half inches long. "This didn't come from any dog that I recognize. It was embedded in Owen's arm. He put up a good fight."

Clay sat down heavily.

"Something sucked the blood from that man." Swenson pointed to the corpse in the next room. "I'm talking vampires and werewolves."

"You're crazy. This whole town's gone nuts."

"Happened before." The doctor rubbed his face with his hands. He rested his head in his palm; his red-rimmed eyes studied Clay.

"There has to be an explanation." Clay said.

"There wasn't then, and there isn't now. I suspect you'll be about ready to call in the FBI."

Clay squirmed on the metal chair. He had been thinking of doing that. "Maybe," he conceded. "I have to talk to the mayor."

"Oh, he's gonna say not to do it. Keep it in the county."

"What happened?" Clay asked.

"Rash of these types of things popped up all over the area. Stopped just as suddenly. The sheriff was Joe Haskell back then. You remember him?"

"How'd he handle it?" Clay's voice was low.

Swenson took a long swig from his flask. "He didn't. Died of a heart attack right in the middle of the investigation. Acting sheriff ended up closing the inquiry. It's in the dead files."

"Huh." Clay nodded, deep in thought.

"Dead files, as in dead and long gone," the doctor muttered.

"Hey, Doc, you ever heard of a family named Bavmorda?"

The older man sat back in his chair; it squeaked from his weight. He leaned back a bit, his lips thinning. "Where'd you hear about the Bavmorda clan?"

"I went to their house today."

The doctor rocked his chair into an upright position. "You did not."

"Yeah, I took the road past the old mill and found Linden Lane at the end of the path."

The doctor took out his pad; his face was concerned. "How long has it been since you slept, Clay." He scribbled something on a prescription and ripped it off the pad. "You've been under a lot of stress . . . well, since Claire and Jenna, of course. No one will think less of you if—"

Clay stood up. "What are you talking about? I swear, this whole place is acting crazy."

The doctor's eyes bored into him. "The Bavmorda place burned down one hundred years ago, killing the entire family. Ain't no house there. Just a bunch of ruins."

Clay hit his hat against his thigh. "I know what I saw." The doctor handed him the script. "Go home to Jenna and get some sleep. Doctor's orders."

10

RABBITS AND DUCKS

Clay dropped into his cruiser wearily. His phone pinged with several messages. Jenna had asked if he was going to come back to her place. That was two hours ago. His body screamed with exhaustion, but he was troubled by his conversation with the doctor. Instead, he circled back to the ever-growing puddle. He determined there were a few gallons more, and pretty soon they'd be calling it a pond.

He drove around the perimeter and followed his route from earlier today. He found the dirt road and traveled up toward the house. The lane went on forever. He didn't remember the house being this far down the path. He stopped his car and got out to search the empty lot. The wind blew around him, rustling the trees. He heard movement, twisting to see Bobby Ray and

Trout walking behind him. They still held that squirming burlap bag.

"What in the hell are you two up to, now?"

"Nuthin'," Bobby Ray answered, swaying on his feet. He sneered at Clay. Clay noticed he was missing several teeth.

"Hunting," Trout mumbled, earning him a jab in the ribs from his cousin.

"What are you hunting out here?" Clay asked. "Ducks," Bobby Ray muttered.

"Rabbits." Trout held up the bag.

Clay watched them both. "Well, which is it?"

This time, Trout shouted, "Ducks!" and Bobby Ray said, "Rabbits."

Clay locked his eyes on the bag. "What happened to the snakes?"

Trout said, "We be done with snakes. You let that one get away from us. Fella's gotta eat. You got a problem with that, Sheriff?"

Clay shook his head. There was no crime in them hunting. Clay didn't trust those two. He peered closely at them. Bobby Ray didn't look too good. He was a ghastly shade of green, and his eyes had sunken into his skull. Clay didn't want to touch anything he was holding.

"You okay?" Clay peered at him closely.

"Touch of the stomach flu," Bobby Ray said.

"Well, then get on home before you infect the entire county." They shuffled off in the other direction. "Hey," Clay called. "You remember where that house was? You know, the Bavmorda house. It's also called the gingerbread house."

Trout nodded. "Yeah, I remember now."

"Great. I can't find it." Clay stood, his hand on his hips.

"'Course you can't. It burnt down a long time ago. Ain't nuthin' there but some old charred wood."

"No, I saw it this morning. I spoke with the woman living there."

Trout laughed, revealing a mouth full of crooked, yellow teeth. "Maybe you got some sort of flu now, Sheriff." Trout walked past him toward a mound of weeds. "Here is the gingerbread house. Right here on this spot."

Clay was annoyed. "Yeah, right." He walked over, his foot banging into a rusted metal bar. He kicked it, but it seemed to be embedded in the soil as if it had been there for a long time. The pole was attached to a mailbox. Bending down, he brushed it off and read the print. Bavmorda Gingerbread House, Linden Lane.

Trout laughed. "See, I tol' you. Nuthin' here but us. Nuthin' at all. Come on, cuz. Let's go."

They loped off toward the old mill on their way back to town. Clay crouched, his fingers brushing the dirt. There were a few broken bricks, a loose roof shingle in a half crescent moon shape as if someone had taken a bite out of it. He kicked it, angry because he didn't understand what was going on. Did he imagine this morning? He wondered. A piece of cotton was attached to a rotted fence post. It fluttered as if it were waving to him. He walked over, his eyes catching a hint of embroidery.

It was a sock, a child's cotton sock, pristine and blindingly white. He plucked it off the wood, snagging it on a splinter. It started to unravel. His head swam; he staggered for a second, his breath coming in great gulps. Bile rushed to the back of his throat, and he fought the urge to throw up. He crushed the tiny sock in his fist, the printed initial scorching an imprint on his hand. He knew those initials: C. F. They were the same as his initials. They were the initials of his daughter, Claire.

11

HOME

He tucked the sock into his breast pocket and got into his cruiser. He turned the car so fast it kicked up a storm of gravel. He wanted to get out of there. His eyes stung with unshed tears, and he wondered if this was a bizarre punishment. His heart was heavy in his chest. All he wanted was Jenna. He needed his wife.

He was tired; he knew he needed to sleep. There was too much going on, and the strange connection with his daughter was driving him crazy.

Clay drove through the giant puddle, not caring if he skirted it. He was too intent on getting to Jenna to care about being cautious. The car sliced through the water like a great white shark. He heard the engine groan. Cursing himself for his stupidity, he pressed the gas, forcing the car to make it though. He passed the older couple's stalled car and roared down the street in the direction of Jenna's condo.

The car had started to sputter by the time he pulled into the complex. Clay was shaking as if he had a fever. He lurched from the car, his legs unsteady. He couldn't focus. As if Jenna knew he was coming, she stood in the doorway, her robe clutched at her neck, her face white with fright.

"Clay, what's wrong?"

He couldn't tell her; he was afraid it would break her heart, send her spiraling back into the dark place where she almost stayed forever. He couldn't lose her again.

He staggered in and would have fallen if she didn't catch him around his middle. "Are you injured?" she asked. She ran her competent hands down his torso. "Tell me where you're hurt."

"I'm all right," his voice came out in a gravelly whisper. "Tired."

"You're dead on your feet. Come on." She helped him into the bedroom. He fell heavily onto the bed. "I can't take your bed." He tried to rise.

Jenna pushed him down. He felt his body go slack. She was bending at the side of the bed, taking off his shoes. He was so tired his eyes felt weighted. He tore at the buttons of his shirt, snagging his fingers on his badge. He heard it thud when it landed on the carpeted floor. He rolled over to grab it, but Jenna pushed him back.

"Leave it. I'll get it later," Jenna told him. She gently removed his hands and unbuttoned his shirt as the world faded to black.

He might have slept for an hour, or he might have been out for a day. Clay opened his eyes, feeling displaced. He didn't know where he was. He felt a soft, warm body pressed up against him.

"Shhh." He heard Jenna say, her small hand resting on his bare chest.

His head fell back; he adjusted his arms to wrap her in his embrace. Her leg was leaning comfortably against his thigh. Jenna was watching him, her eyes shining in the darkness. He lowered his head, capturing her lips. Their tongues met, and Clay groaned at their touch. He felt her flesh burning through her nightgown against his bare chest. His heart pounded in tandem with hers, as if the two organs were doing a duet. He leaned over and kissed her there, healing her heart. She grabbed his face, their tongues lacing together, the dance familiar and comforting. The world around Clay receded until all he felt was Jenna's mouth.

Jenna grabbed his pants buckle frantically; he helped by shucking off his pants, then his underwear. He lifted her above him, settling her on top of him. She was as desperate as he, their need to be closer making their hands fumble clumsily. Jenna wrapped him in her moist heat, grinding in a primal movement that made him shout with desire.

He ripped her nightgown, exposing her breasts, pulling her down to bury his face in her flesh, his mouth searching and finding a nipple. He heard her sobbing, and, cupping her face tenderly, he whispered, "I missed you . . . I love you."

He bucked upward, feeling her close around him. They moved together, their hands joined as well, the intimacy of their palms touching more erotic than any other part of their body.

He growled her name. Nothing mattered but the two of them. Flipping her over, his head buried in the valley where her neck met her shoulder, Clay murmured that he loved her, that she was everything to him.

She answered with a sigh as she found her release. Clay followed her with an intensity that left him feeling one with the stars.

Jenna pulled him to her. He rolled over, tucking her under his shoulder, and they slept entwined.

Clay woke to an empty bed. He sat up, located his underwear and went to the bathroom. He rested his palms on the sink. He needed a shave. He opened Jenna's medicine cabinet to look for an unused razor and reared back when he found not only a man's razor but a bottle of aftershave as well. He sniffed the cologne. It was unfamiliar to him. Who did it belong to? He closed the mirrored door, his heart plummeting.

Jenna was in the kitchen, her back straight. He could tell by her stance that she was angry. Words clogged in his throat.

She placed a black coffee in front of him, her lips taut in a grim line.

She sat opposite him, her hand fisted. She opened it, letting the sock roll from her palm onto the small table she used for meals.

Tears leaked from her shadowed, blue eyes. "This is Claire's. Where did you get it?"

She began to sob then, and Clay rose to take her in his arms, all questions about the strange aftershave forgotten. "I found it on Linden Lane. I'll find her. I promise you, Jenna. I will find Claire."

12

HELLO, DOLLY

Dolly looked up when he entered the office, their eyes meeting. Dolly's silvery hair was in a neat bun above her friendly, round face. She was somewhere over sixty. Clay wasn't sure how old she was and would never think of asking her age. She was a fixture in Bulwark, as much a part of the tapestry of the town as Main Street. He couldn't remember a time when she wasn't a part of his life. He remembered trick-or-treating at her small house on Halloween when he was a kid. Now they worked together as colleagues. Either way, he couldn't recall her without the tidy silver bun and kind dark eyes. She had been old his entire life, and this was not going to be an easy conversation. Truth be told, sometimes she scared the crap out of him, with her biting remarks and stern admonishment. Today, he was angry. This somehow involved Claire. He loomed over her, feeling slightly guilty when she cowered in her chair.

"Did you know about Linden Lane?" he asked, forcing a calm he didn't feel into his voice. His heart pounded as though it would burst from his chest. He knew she had the answers. The silence thickened between them.

She gulped then looked down, her lips tightening.

"Dolly!" he whispered fiercely, bending down to meet her, eye to eye. Gripping her narrow shoulders and feeling their frailness, he eased his hold. "Did you know what I would find?"

She looked up, her eyes darting around as if she was afraid. "You'll never believe me." Her voice was a mere thread.

"Try me."

"Not here," she said, with a look of warning.

Clay glanced around the empty room. Dolly looked pointedly at the doorway where the rest of the staff worked. "Sherri's in there. Terence called in sick."

"Again?" Clay ground out. "I'm shorthanded."

"Sherri said he was white as a ghost."

Clay conceded that Dolly was right. Terence looked horrible yesterday. He called for his deputy. "Sherri, head out to the hospital and see the accident victim, that guy

Henry. See if he can talk yet. Try to get a statement."

Sherri poked her head in the room. She looked from Clay's set face to Dolly's nervous one. "Everything okay in here?"

"I need that statement," Clay told her.

"I'm on it." Sherri placed her hat on her head and bounded out the door.

Clay stalked to his office and sat down in his chair. Dolly followed him into the room. He pointed to the seat in front of him. "Okay, we're alone now."

Dolly sank onto the metal seat, her lips pursed. "I don't know where to start."

"Start at the beginning."

"It's a long story, Clay."

Clay looked at his watch, murmuring. "I'll make time for this." He tapped his foot impatiently.

The older woman shrugged. "You may find it . . . hard to swallow."

"I'll refrain from making any comments."

Dolly cleared her throat and started. "In 1764 . . ."

Clay sat up abruptly, "What . . . 1764? Are you kidding me?"

"Do you want me to tell you or not?" Dolly snapped. "You promised you wouldn't make any comments."

Clay held up his hands in surrender. "I'm mute, Doll. Go ahead."

"The Bavmordas settled the land east of Bulwark in 1764. They were from an aristocratic family, emigrating from England. The mother was tried and burned as a witch back in Europe, but the family escaped . . ."

Clay interrupted again. "Witches. I swear you and Doc are crazy. Him with his werewolves and vampires, and you with your witches."

"I thought you said you were mute, so sit down and shut up."

This time he smirked. That was the Dolly of his youth. "Okay. Go ahead."

"As I was saying, the mother was burned at the stake as a witch in England. The son and wife escaped to the colonies. There were rumors about them. Strange things were going on. People steered clear of them."

Clay shrugged. "We've had our share of weirdos in the area. Remember Bobby Ray Parker's great-uncle?"

"That was just white-trash shenanigans. The Bavmordas were different. Wicked."

"If that's so, why didn't I ever hear about them or their history? This town is full of old stories about the strange goings on in some of the families. There's always talk."

"You can thank the town council. They had everything stricken from the record. The town leadership had this theory that talking about the Bavmorda clan gave the family the power to do wicked things."

Clay raised his eyebrows. He rose to pace the room. "Hmm . . . wicked things?"

Dolly held up a wrinkled hand. "Yes, wicked things." She met Clay's doubtful eyes and added, "I swear. It's the truth. You want me to finish the story?"

Clay nodded and sat on the edge of his cluttered desk. He shoved a stack of papers. They tipped and spilled over the surface of his desk. He was thoughtful as he considered the older woman. Dolly represented the best of Bulwark. If she said something, Clay had to admit, he needed to take it seriously. He shrugged, hoping it was not the beginning of senility. How old was she, anyway? He wondered.

"It was said they were evil folks. They didn't mix with the rest of the town. Strange things happened around here. Unexplainable things."

"Like what?" Clay was still not convinced.

"People would disappear. Usually vagrants, sometimes a teen."

"That's an old story, Dolly. Every town has shit like that happen. You can't blame it on a family just because they didn't like to socialize with others."

"There's more. The legend is that they had a child, and it died. The wife went crazy."

Clay shifted in his seat. His child disappeared. Jenna had a breakdown. "Life isn't always good. Bad things happen to people. It doesn't make them evil. Sounds like the town wasn't exactly compassionate."

"Oh," she added as she remembered things. "They had hounds. Some called them hellhounds."

Clay snorted. "Is that the best you've got?"

"I'm just telling you what I know. They say the old witch never got old. She bathed in the blood of her victims."

"So, she bathed in the blood, but didn't drink it." His voice had an edge of sarcasm. "Why blood?"

"I don't know, but that's how she washed. Maybe she drank it too."

"So, was she a vampire and a witch?"

"Who said anything about a vampire? Just because someone drinks blood, it doesn't make them a vampire. That's just a bunch of nonsense. People disappeared, I told you. Mostly servants or homeless drifters, that kind of thing. People didn't care enough to do something. Fear kept them from stopping them." Her voice turned into a whisper. "Every so often an infant disappeared."

Clay became alert. "An infant goes missing, and the law didn't pursue it?"

"There were investigations. They were acquitted. There was no evidence, you see."

Clay cursed.

"Look, Clay, fear blinds people. They see what they want to see. They believe what they need to in order to survive."

"I still don't understand why I've never heard about this? Especially because of Claire." He looked at her, his eyes hurt.

"I don't know. It hasn't happened for a long time. People want to forget what they can't fix," Dolly said in a rush. "Anyway, the family line died out. The house burned down. That's about it."

Clay studied Dolly's face, his jaw set. He'd bet his best fishing pole she was hiding something.

"Out with it, Doll."

Dolly lowered her eyes from Clay's gaze. "Now!"

"They say she comes back every fifty years. She needs fresh blood to stay young and beautiful, so she takes children. Steals them and keeps them."

"Okay!" He stood, his chair flying backward. "That's enough. Claire was taken a year ago, not fifty years ago."

Dolly placed her face on her hands. "She comes back every fifty years and stays for the twelve months. Very few can see her." She looked up, her eyes distant as if she saw an invisible tableau. "But, oh, she is there, and she is sending out her minions to stock her house for the next fifty years."

"How do you know?" Clay demanded.

Dolly paused, took a deep breath and replied, "I escaped her clutches. My twin didn't."

"What?"

"Fifty-one years ago. My sister and I were playing in a field, near my dad's farm." She gestured her hand vaguely. "The trees started to weep. It was a weird phenomenon they attributed to changes in the climate. They bled murky, dark stuff and wouldn't stop. It created a river blocking the street. That green water cut us off from town. Bavmorda's an old lady until she replenishes. She lured us in with the promise of candy. Back then, we didn't know it was wrong to take candy from strangers."

The room was quiet, her voice the barest whisper. "There was a boy on the roof. She told us her house was made of gingerbread. He was standing there, eating a roof shingle. My sister . . . she wanted to try it. The woman said the walls were made of icing. The doorknobs were clusters of gumdrops. You know . . . like Hansel and Gretel. I asked her if she was a witch. The old lady laughed at me. She made me feel silly. She said there was no such thing as witches."

Dolly's eyes were far away again, as if she were seeing the scene played out before her.

"I wish I could turn back time. . . . We went into that house, foolish, greedy children that we were. It was a trap. A boy locked us in cages. There must have been dozens of us. Kids, all kids locked in cages." Dolly's arthritic fingers gripped Clay's knee. She spoke urgently. Clay didn't think to question her. He wasn't listening anymore. All he could think about was Claire. Dolly went on, more to herself than the sheriff. "I escaped, though. I got out, but too late to save my sister. Too late."

Clay looked up, a new question entering his mind. "The accident victim—the woman said the witch looked like JB's wife."

Dolly shook her head. "She can change her appearance. I thought she looked like my grandmother when I met her. My sister said she looked like the preacher's wife."

Clay nodded. "She looked like Mrs. Emmerson to me."

She sighed then and looked at Clay. "So, do you believe me now?"

"Why didn't you say anything?"

"I couldn't. The mayor, the sheriff . . . even the doctor swore me to silence. He said they would lock me up in an asylum if I talked. My mother made me promise never to open my mouth. They made up a story about my sister, saying she drowned, and, after a while, I started to believe it too. If you say something often enough, it becomes the truth."

"How could you not tell me when Claire went missing?" Clay's voice was strangled.

"It had been so many years . . . and Claire was young. The legend was that she took older children. I thought a drifter probably did it."

"No, she's got Claire." Clay was sure of it.

Dolly nodded. "Probably that couple's children too. You know, the accident victims from Atlanta." Dolly gripped his arm. "Listen to me, Clay, there is nothing you can do."

He stood up. "Yes, there is. You escaped, and I'm going to get Claire out of there." He took her hand and pulled her from the room.

Dolly followed and replied, "If she's still alive. Where are you taking me?"

"We're going to the gingerbread house."

13

"I WON'T GO BACK THERE"

"I won't go back there!" Dolly turned from the entrance of the building. Clay stood up abruptly and yanked the door open. Dayna Dalton landed on the floor. Clay hauled her up by the shoulders. She molded herself against him, wrapping her arms around his neck.

Clay reached up to pull her off of him, only to hear a gasp of dismay. Jenna stood in the doorway holding his badge. Her other hand was in front of her mouth, her eyes filled with tears. She extended a shaking hand. "This fell off. I thought you would need it." She choked and threw the badge at them. It bounced off his shoulder harmlessly. He pushed Dayna aside, who snickered and followed Jenna out the station.

"Jenna," he called. "Come back. It's not what you think."

But she took off in her Jetta, her face wet with tears. Clay stood torn, wanting to follow and explain but knowing he had to find the gingerbread house and Claire. Ignoring Dayna, he grabbed Dolly by the wrist.

Dayna raced after him shouting, "This time you're not leaving without me."

Clay spun, his face filled with rage. "Stay out of this, Dayna. Stay away, or I'll arrest you." He opened the door for Dolly, and then looked at the reporter, his face hard. "I mean it." He got into the other side of the car and left, sending a cloud of dust into the thick air.

They drove toward the puddle. It was noticeably smaller. Dolly sucked air into her lungs. "She's leaving."

"What?" Clay demanded.

Dolly pointed to the water that now covered less than half the street. "The water's receding. She doesn't need it anymore, the barrier to protect her. She will soon disappear for another fifty years."

"No, she won't!" Clay drove through the water. His windshield was covered with the greenish muck. His wipers smeared the slime so that he had trouble seeing outside.

They passed the old mill. The empty buildings looked as if they were enveloped in a mist. Clay opened the windows, and the car filled with the sound of howls.

"The hellhounds. They'll rip us to shreds."

"At least they're not werewolves. Hellhounds I can handle." He stepped on the gas. The car took off, fishtailing, then straightened as they raced down Linden Lane.

"Don't be a smart-ass, Clay. They're as real as I am." Dolly grabbed his arm. "Clay!"

A figure stumbled from the fog, his hands outstretched. Clay slammed the brakes, squinting in the gloom. The man was familiar. It couldn't be him. He was home. Terence was home and sick.

Dolly's voice squeaked, "It's Terence!"

The figure staggered closer. Indeed, it was Terence, Clay confirmed. He looked as if he was dragging himself toward them, his eyes blood-red, his face a fish-belly white. "What's wrong with him? He looks like a zombie!" Clay was shocked.

"She has protectors. People who fall under her spell."

"Okay, I've had just about enough of this."

"Clay." Dolly's fingers dug into the skin of his arm. "They have powers. She is able somehow to make them invulnerable."

"Terence never saw her," Clay shouted. "If this is all true, the whole town's involved."

"She picks outsiders who help her. Anyone who gets in their way is killed or controlled."

Clay reached back and grabbed his shotgun. "We'll see about that."

Clay got out of the car and planted himself in front of the vehicle. "Stop where you are, Terence."

The young cop ignored him and continued lurching in his direction. Clay had to admit the kid looked creepy, all pasty-looking and vacant. "I said stop right there, Terence. I don't want to hurt you." The rookie looked through him as if he didn't see Clay. Clay stepped toward him, determined to stop him without injuring the younger man. Whatever was going on with him, he didn't want to see anything dire happen to him. "Terence, I'm warning you." Clay reached forward, using the barrel of the gun to prevent Terence from getting closer. The young man plucked the gun from Clay's hands and tossed it away like a toy. They grappled for a minute. Clay was surprised by the iron grip of Terence's fingers. In the past, he had dismissed the rookie as a lightweight. Sweat dripped from Clay's brow. He was working hard, evading the erratic fists pummeling him. It was as if he were fighting a machine. Terence managed to block his punches while delivering a punishing attack splitting the skin over his eyebrow. Clay was breathing hard. The cut above his eye throbbed. He was dizzy, and he must have swayed on his feet, but he fought on.

Terence kicked out, sending Clay into the hard-packed dirt. He hit his head on a rock; sound receded for a second. He forced himself to his wobbly knees, made a single fist with one hand, and surged upward. Clay connected with Terence's jaw. The smack reverberated up Clay's arms. He felt his teeth rattle. Terence rocked back, then pushed forward, his hands wrapping around Clay's neck, his thumbs pressing against his windpipe. Stars danced before Clay's eyes— not in a good way, he thought hazily. Clay forced his leaden arms to circle under his captor's grip to push outward, breaking Terence's hold, sending them both staggering backward.

Clay landed in the dirt, falling on his back with a dull thud. A shadow loomed over him. He scrambled to his feet. Terence hooked him under his jaw and started lifting him with inhuman strength. Clay choked as he pounded the young officer's shoulder with a fist that was growing weaker by the minute.

Clay looked sadly down the long road, and the air sparkled and shimmered. He could see the Victorian house appear. It was no longer dilapidated. The clapboards gleamed white; the roof was a marvel of reddish roof tile, the chimneys smoked with welcome.

Clay's eyes dimmed with sadness. He wasn't going to reach Claire. He watched in a detached manner as Dolly picked up the shotgun, approaching stealthily behind Terence. With a swing that would have made A-Rod proud, she whacked Terence on the side of his unsuspecting head. His eyes rolled up, and he slid bonelessly to the ground, taking Clay with him.

Clay lay stunned on the ground. Dolly grabbed him under his armpits and yelled, "We have to hurry! The house, it's changing already."

Clay's feet slipped out from under him. Using the heel of his palm, he pushed up, then fell again. He rose unsteadily to his feet and ran to the car. Dolly slid into the seat, slamming the door. He gunned the engine and took off in the direction of the looming mansion.

It wavered in the air, blinking in and out. One second the lot was empty; the next, the gleaming Victorian took shape. Clay's car raced up the drive, Dolly's urgent cries filled the vehicle.

The car screeched to a halt, swerving as the house materialized again. Clay got out of the car as two figures emerged from the front door. He saw a third on the roof. Bobby Ray and Trout walked down the front steps, their faces filled with a strange light. Clay stared at Trout's lowered brows—his usually dull eyes narrowed. They looked different, as if they belonged to someone else, and, for a minute, he wondered if the color of his eyes had changed.

Bobby Ray slowed, and Trout came up next to him, stretching their arms over their heads. The sky above turned dark and moody; thunder boomed in the background, and a bolt of electricity split the horizon. Bobby Ray was chanting, a slow, monotonous sound, his face rapt. He fell to his knees as Clay moved to stand in front of the car. He heard Dolly scream, "No, Clay!"

The two cousins fell on all fours, howling like wild dogs. The light blinked as if the power went out on the planet. Day became night. Clay watched the men change their forms, becoming indistinct. Hair sprouted all over their bodies; they stretched their necks as the light shifted. Their outlines morphed from human to canine.

"The hellhounds!" Dolly reached for him, urging him back to the car.

Clay stood frozen, his breath caught in his chest. He pulled his gun, aiming. "Where's my daughter!" he growled at the same time the beasts howled back. They snarled, saliva drooling from their ferocious snouts, crouching low, ready to strike. He fired then, the shots harmlessly going through the creatures as though they didn't exist.

Clay looked at his gun then fired another round. Nothing. The bullets had no effect on the creatures.

"I want him alive!" said the man standing on the roof as he jumped to land between Clay and the beasts. "I want to see him suffer." He walked over, his manner sly and devious. He was dressed in clothes from another era, homespun and old fashioned. A felt hat shadowed his face. Clay recognized the garments from the medieval fairs that frequented the area. He shot his gun again, the bullets pinging harmlessly against the clapboard of the house.

"Your weapon is useless," the man snarled, moving closer. Clay stood firmly, holding his ground. The stranger lifted his hat, and Clay's jaw dropped. Dr. Peter Kent smiled evilly at him.

"What are you doing here?" Clay held the gun pointed at the young doctor.

Kent walked to Clay, their chests almost touching. He pushed his face directly underneath Clay's, as if to intimidate him. Clay felt himself freeze. He couldn't move, even if he wanted to. It was as if some invisible force field held him captive.

Peter Kent took the gun from Clay's grip. Raising his hands, the doctor snapped his fingers. The beasts pounced, and Clay knew nothing more.

14

A CELLAR OF HORRORS

Clay groaned deep in his chest, every muscle aching. He tried to roll up but realized he couldn't move. Rope bound him. He was hogtied, his ankles tethered behind him to his wrists. He pulled, bucking against the ropes.

"Save your strength," he heard a voice say weakly. He looked up to find Dolly crouched in a small cage, not unlike the kind used to keep pets. They were in a darkened cellar, a hard-packed earthen floor underneath them. Clay looked up at the blackened joists holding up the level above them. The ceiling hung low, like a root cellar. He knew that if he rose up, he couldn't stand upright. Picking up his heavy head, he looked around. A single bulb swayed overhead, casting light in the dim interior. Steamer trunks, barrels, and piles of junk took up a good half of the room. He and the rest of the prisoners were squeezed into a small area; the air was damp and musty. Clay coughed, spitting out dirt.

"You okay?" His voice sounded gravelly. Dolly shrugged, her eyes large in her face.

"How come I'm not in one of those?" He gestured to the row of pens holding people.

"They tried. You didn't fit." Dolly laughed without humor. "They couldn't get your shoulders through."

Clay wiggled a bit, his ribs and shoulders screaming from pain. He grunted. "They must have tried very hard."

"You were not cooperative," Dolly said. "This is where they kept me before."

They heard a baby's cry echoed in the house. Clay struggled wildly to get free. "Claire?" he whispered.

"It might be. They're getting ready to leave."

"How do you know?"

Dolly motioned to another row of cages. They were stacked on top of one another, each filled with strangers. There must have been fifteen people in there, all different ages, but most were of small stature and looked starved. Clay saw they were huddled in their space, catatonic, hunched, and emaciated. He realized the room smelled as if something had died. There was the overwhelming odor of human waste.

"They took out a boy. I recognized him. He was the runaway who panhandled down at the train station. You know, you picked him up once for vagrancy."

Clay made a sound. "And here I thought my superior policing policies were keeping the runaways from staying in our town. Where is he?"

The lights flickered above them and Clay searched the dim interior to see Dolly looking at him. "She's building her power. She's beginning her sacrifices."

He glanced at the prisoners, noting that they seemed confused, or even trance-like. Some were mumbling, others appeared catatonic, but Clay recognized horror and disbelief. "We'll get out of here," he called to them. There was no reaction. If anything, they appeared to shrink before his eyes. "How did you get out the last time?"

Dolly didn't answer. He heard the baby wail and pulled at his restraints with renewed force. Inching over to the nearest cage, he called to a stringy-haired girl squeezed into the corner. On the floor of her cage she had the remains of food; her eyes were blank.

"Hey." He tried to get her to focus on him. He rolled over so that his back was to her. "Untie the rope." He held his bound fists up to the bars separating them.

She ignored him, her head resting on her knee.

"Help me. We'll escape."

"Can you move to me?" a reedy voice called from behind.

Clay peered into the dim interior. The speaker seemed far off. Clay crawled his way painfully; his skin rubbed raw by the hard floor. There was a row of cages, each with a single occupant. Most of them were grubby teens, the kind he was always writing up for sleeping on park benches or in the bus depot.

"Who said they'd help?" he asked hoarsely.

A bony finger beckoned him. Clay moved toward it, biting his lips until they bled. It was a teen, his face familiar. He couldn't place him, though. He backed himself against the cage and felt the fumbling fingers work the rope, the boy's grimy hands digging into his skin. The binds loosened, then gave away. Clay unclasped the cage, and the boy squeezed out as Clay got to his feet, his head grazing the beams. His body screamed with agony. The boy looked as if he would faint. He had no color in his face. Clay steadied the boy when he wobbled. Together, they released the springs on the other cages, helping the weakened prisoners from their confines. Clay unlatched Dolly's cage and helped her stand. The baby cried again. "Dolly, you stay here and organize them." His voice was urgent. He looked and saw the boy hugging a girl tenderly. He was brushing the matted hair from her face.

Clay approached them. "We have to get out of here." He considered the girl's blank stare. "Is she okay?"

"This is my sister, she . . . they scared her. She needs to go home. We're from Atlanta. We were checking out colleges." He shrugged. "She didn't want to stop here. She didn't like your town."

Clay nodded. "I don't blame her. Have you seen any way out other than the stairs?"

The boy pointed to each corner of the room. "We're in a basement. I've counted four windows."

Clay looked at the filthy glass, shaking his head. The windows were nailed shut. He rubbed a spot to see outside. A dark shadow loped by. The dogs, or whatever they claimed to be, were guarding the windows. He moved toward a bench. It was cluttered with garden equipment. He grabbed a pair of long shears, tossing them to the boy, who caught them easily. "Think you can use those?"

"Jacob. My name is Jacob." Clay saw him nod in the darkness.

Clay picked up a pitchfork and hefted it in his hands. He would make it work. The baby screamed. Clay gave the stairs a worried look. "Okay, Jacob, let's go kick some butt."

"You'll take care of my sister." Jacob looked at Dolly. "Her name is Lydia." He turned and patted her hand. "I'll come back, Lydie, and we'll go home."

Dolly scrambled over and put her arm around the girl. "We'll be just fine here. We're ready to leave as soon as you give us the say so. We're going to wait for you and then we'll all leave together." She looked at Clay, who inclined his head. "Go find Claire, and let's get out of here." The dazed prisoners moved closer to Dolly, who held her arms out as if to embrace them all. She murmured comforting sounds, clucking and soothing.

Clay rooted around a few boxes, coming away with a crowbar, a wrench, and a spade. There was a roll of duct tape. He chucked it to Jacob. He grabbed an ax in his other hand. Dolly swayed on her feet. He steadied her, found a bucket, and overturned it. He pushed the old woman onto the makeshift seat. He handed out the weapons, saving the crowbar for Dolly. "You know what to do?"

"Believe me, I know exactly what to do."

The door hinges squealed loudly, causing the group to hold their collective breaths. Clay directed them to back away, his pointer finger covering his lips, indicating silence. The crowd melted into the shadows as Bobby Ray descended the basement steps.

Clay motioned for Jacob to go to the other side of the dingy room. They heard Bobby Ray's voice as he muttered to himself about slop and feeding time. He stood at the base of the steps, squinting into the gloom, holding a bucket of gunk. The smell was noxious, filling the cellar with the heavy odor of decay. Bobby Ray's eyes appeared to adjust, and he walked toward the rows of cages. Clay waited until he brushed his shoulder, then sprang from the darkness, jumping him. He grabbed him from behind, smothering his cry with his hand. Bobby Ray struggled against him, but Clay held him firmly.

"Where's Claire?" Clay demanded.

Bobby Ray's eye's widened until the whites surrounded the irises. He shook his head.

Clay spun him around, grasping him under the chin, so Bobby Ray's face purpled as he gasped for air.

"Do you know where she is?" Clay squeezed his neck harder. Bobby Ray's chest heaved. "Do you?" He hissed under his breath.

Bobby Ray nodded.

"You're going to take us there." Clay snapped for Jacob to throw him the duct tape. Using his teeth, he ripped off a long strip, winding it around Bobby Ray's face, knowing it would tear every hair from his head when he took it off. He pushed him toward the steps, their bodies so close he could smell Bobby Ray's foul stink. They climbed the staircase, their bodies hugging the wall, the pitchfork clumsy under his arm.

Clay gave the signal for Jacob to open the door. It creaked as he opened it, he winced at the loud squeak. Clay watched as Jacob poked his head out. There was a tense minute. Bobby Ray bucked, hitting his head on the wall. Clay pressed the ax under his chin, shaving off a layer of whiskers. "You move again like that, and I'll lop off your head and bring it to your mama." Bobby Ray's eyes were round as saucers. He nodded with understanding. Clay could feel him quaking, his muscles bunching as if he would flee as soon as they got through the door. He pushed Bobby Ray into the opening and whispered close to his ear. "I'll shove this pitchfork so far up your ass, you'll sound like a flute when you fart." He brandished it at him.

They heard a woman singing down a hall. The corridor was layered in shadows that danced on the walls. Clay shuffled along, trying to keep as quiet as he could. Doorways lined the hall. At each opening he dragged his prisoner past the portal, releasing a pent-up breath as they bypassed the entrances to the different rooms of the house. The singing grew louder. It was a young woman's voice. She sounded carefree, her songs filling the halls.

BULWARK

Clay peered into a room that was lit full of sunshine. A white cradle stood in the corner; he could see a blonde cap of hair, a chubby leg, a dimpled fist. The room spun for a second, and he heard the child babble. Dots danced before his eyes, and he must have loosened his hold because Bobby Ray slipped out of his grip. He tore at the duct tape, frantically pulling out skin and hair, screaming, "Watch out, Miss B. He's got a weapon!"

The woman spun, her hair whipping around her head. She was holding a child. His child. The room tilted, and, for a minute, Clay swayed. The little girl looked at him quizzically then held out her arms and said, "Da." The woman placed her in the large crib, waved her arms, and a sparkling protective net appeared out of thin air and dropped around Claire, imprisoning her.

She didn't look like the old hag who opened the door yesterday. This woman had red hair and smooth skin. Her face was familiar. The green eyes twitched, and Clay stared into the face of Dayna Dalton.

"You wouldn't hurt an old friend, would you, Clay?" she asked, her hips swaying as she moved closer. Jacob entered the room, brandishing his shears. Dayna's face contorted. She pointed to Bobby Ray and said something in a language Clay didn't understand. Bobby Ray fell to his knees,

94

letting out a howl. His body shifted into that of a silver hound, front paws springing forward to attack.

"You're not Dayna!"

"Maybe." Her laughter bounced off the walls. "Are you seeing me or who you want to see? Do you want to see a witch? A wicked witch?" The air shimmered around the woman, and sparks flew through the room. She started to shrink, her skin turning a nasty shade of green, shriveling like a prune. Her body folded inward, her eyes becoming deep pits of hatred, her mouth a slash of crimson. She started reciting something. Her maw opened, a loud roar escaping her lips coupled with a mighty wind.

It blasted Clay; he brandished the pitchfork at her. The witch threw back her head and cackled. Behind them, Claire shrieked with fear. She rolled into a ball and cowered in the corner of the cradle.

Jacob shoved Clay out of the way, rushing forward with a loud scream. With both hands he snapped the shears, the clacking making Claire wail louder.

Clay shook his head, then aimed the pitchfork at Bavmorda. She placed her gnarled hands in front of her face. A forked tongue projected from her mouth, lashing Clay with a poisonous sting. Welts erupted on his skin where it touched him. It felt as if he were rolling in a field of nettles. She hissed, her tongue so fast it was like fencing with a master. She chuckled again. "You're so predictable. This is boring me." The air shimmered and sparkled. He was looking at Jenna's tearful gaze. He froze, his arms immobilized.

"What do you see now, Clay?"

Clay shook his head as if to clear it. He swayed dizzily. Jacob grabbed the ax, and when he raised it to strike the witch, Clay held out his arms. "It's my wife!" Clay took the ax and threw it at the wall. It thudded into the plaster.

"No, it's not." Jacob fought with him. "It's a spell."

Jenna turned to pick up the baby. Claire calmed and wrapped her chubby arms around Jenna. He stared, his jaw slack. Claire was comfortable with her. It was Jenna. She pushed past him as she escaped the room, the baby watching him, her blue eyes wide. Clay heard her call as she walked out the door, "Finish them off."

The panting animal lunged, its long teeth clamping on Clay's arm like a vice. He fell to his knees, the hot scent of the creature's breath on his cheek. He pounded the dog's head with his good hand but felt the lights dimming.

Through a red haze, he saw Jacob come at the dog, his hedge clippers snapping at its neck. The animal turned, snapping at him, catching the teen's thigh in a vice-like hold. Jacob paled and stabbed down, the shears doing little damage. Clay found the pitchfork and rammed it into the beast's back. It sliced through the flesh, sending a geyser of blood in the air. The dog whirled, its massive paws landing on Clay, pushing him to the floor, the jaws aiming for his exposed neck. He tried to roll, but the bleeding animal trapped him. Clay saw Jacob run to the wall, grab the ax by the wooden handle, then swing it in a wide arc. The beast's head flew from its body, hitting the wall with a dull thud. The twitching body sprawled atop Clay, smothering him.

Clay was on the floor, a puddle of blood forming around him. Bobby Ray's twitching body lay sprawled on top of him. He was no longer a beast. His head lay on the floor, his eyes sightless. Clay extricated his arm from under the corpse. His uniform was shredded. His limb was a mass of bites, his skin torn. He flexed his hand painfully then pushed himself to a sitting position. The room reeled around him. Clay got weakly to his feet, grabbed the pitchfork, and rushed from the chamber.

They skirted the corridors, stopping dead in their tracks in the front parlor. Dr. Kent, Jenna, and his daughter stood together as if they were a family.

"No!" he shouted, running toward them.

15

BAVMORDA

Clay barreled into Dr. Kent, head-butting him. They fell back in a tangle of limbs. The two men rolled on the floor, Kent on top. Clay felt himself losing strength. Blood loss from the dog bites and the abuse his body had been through had taken its toll. Kent had the pitchfork in both hands, holding it horizontally, pushing down the wooden handle to clamp it under Clay's chin.

Clay resisted, his arms shook from the strain. He saw the creature pretending to be Jenna looking down at him. "Poor, poor Clay. Just give in. Stop struggling," she soothed. She rocked the baby in her arms as she strolled around the perimeters of the parlor. "Trout!" she called. "Trout, come help your master!"

Jacob burst into the room threatening them with his shears. "Ha!" Bavmorda laughed. Clay refused to think of her as Jenna.

She placed the sleeping baby on the sofa, raised her hands, flicking them in Jacob's direction. There was a crackle of electricity, the smell of ozone. The boy was thrown against the wall, his shears flying from his hands.

"Have you finished yet?" the witch asked.

Clay saw her watching his fight with Kent, tapping her foot on the floor impatiently. "What did one of my sisters say? Oh yes, 'If you want something said, give it to a man. If you want something done, then give it to a woman,'" she huffed at Dr. Kent. "You're a useless troll, and you should look like one."

Kent cursed; he shook from the effort of trying to strangle Clay. He jerked back for a second, his eyes widening, his skin changing in texture, becoming pitted and wrinkled. His body seemed to contract into itself, his legs becoming short stumps, his hands long, claw-like things. "Just get off him!" Bavmorda screamed at Kent. "I'll take care of it."

Clay felt himself being lifted and thrown against the wall next to Jacob. They hung in midair while Bavmorda approached them.

"You'll be a tasty morsel." She considered Jacob. She walked over to Clay, appraising him, her hand caressing his leg. "You, I might keep around for a while."

The troll grunted. He got on his stunted legs and walked drunkenly over to the witch. "You . . ." She pointed to him. ". . . bore me. I'm tired of you." She snapped her fingers, and the troll vanished.

She moved closer to Clay. He was caught in an invisible web against the wall. Her voice was a purr. "Nice. I'm in need of a new . . . pool boy."

"Why did you take my child?" He forced the words from his mouth.

"Mine was taken, stolen from her cradle by the sanctimonious people of Bulwark. They said I was an unfit mother!" She twirled and pointed a finger at Claire, who lay sleeping on the couch. "Does she look as though she's suffered?" she demanded. "Does she?"

"You had no right!" Clay strained against the forces holding him. He vibrated with hatred. "You ruined my life, destroyed my marriage, hurt my wife!"

Bavmorda laughed, her wicked chuckle incongruous with Jenna's angelic face. Clay couldn't look her in the eye. He felt her studying him, and when he looked up, she was someone else. Slender, with dark hair and hard green eyes. The round face, the shape of her nose, the smooth skin, stirred a memory he couldn't place. Clay furrowed his brow. She must have read his mind, because she said, "This is me, the real me. This is what I want to look like. Do you understand now?"

Clay's face registered only revulsion. "No. There's no excuse for what you do, Bavmorda."

"It's all in your Bible. An eye for an eye, you foolish man. Your townspeople took my child away. They changed her, made her into a model citizen, altered the direction of her life so that she became one of you, instead of like her own people."

"That happened hundreds of years ago, in another time. That was done by others. You can't take what is not yours."

"I replaced what was taken from me."

"You have no right to continue this vendetta or use people for your own horrific needs." He looked her straight in her eyes and spat, "Your child has been dead and buried for years now, anyway."

"No, she isn't." Dolly stood at the entrance of the room, her hair undone. The gray masses were heavy on her shoulders. She seemed taller, as if she'd grown additional inches. Her back was straight, her face fierce and angry. Her eyes burned with an inner fire. She had an elegance Clay had never seen before.

Bavmorda backed away, her hand on her chest. "Who are you?"

"You know who I am, Mother. You were a careless parent. You let me go, many,

many times." Dolly threw back her head and snarled.

Clay stared slack-jawed. Dolly didn't resemble the old woman he'd worked with all those years. She was suddenly a stranger to him, and while her face showed its maturity, she glowed. "What about your sister? The story you told me?" Clay glared at Dolly as if he'd never seen her.

"It was all lies. I came here to see her. I come every fifty years, waiting for her bloodlust to be sated. She's the one who left me all those years ago—Left me to rot while people around me aged and died. She abandoned me here to live in purgatory. The townspeople didn't take me away." She turned burning eyes on Clay. "She threw me out like yesterday's trash. Took another girl, every fifty years coming back to steal someone's else's daughter, rejecting me for different humans because I wasn't good enough." Dolly walked into the room. She was graceful, not the arthritic old woman he'd known his whole life.

"Are you telling me . . ." Clay asked in a strangled voice.

Dolly shook her head. "Whatever she is, I just wanted to come home."

"Yes, I remember you now," said the witch. "You're ugly, dumpy. You became one of them."

"And if I did, it was because you rejected me."

"You had no future. You never understood why we do what we do." She walked around Dolly, studying her. "I should have recognized you. You look like your father. I didn't like him either. I should have drowned you when I had the chance."

Dolly held out her hand in supplication. "Why didn't you want me?"

"Dolly!" Clay yelled. "She's a murderer. She kills people for their blood."

Dolly ignored Clay, her eyes on her mother. "Why didn't you take me back?" she wailed.

"You were weak. Couldn't do a spell if your life depended on it. The blood repulsed you. You wouldn't use it the way we needed, the way we do to stay young and pretty." Bavmorda studied her like an insect. "I left you by the water, you know, floating on the lake. I was hoping the basket would overturn and let the water finish the job. I took a new child every time I came back, but none of them worked out." She looked at the sleeping baby and sighed. "I was looking for a daughter, one willing to learn." She shook her head. "They never really learn. It must be the DNA. But they come in handy when I find myself hungry."

Clay struggled against the invisible manacles gluing him to the wall. He banged his arms and legs, but he was stuck fast.

"You were never satisfied. I was never good enough for you," Dolly snarled.

"True, dear." Bavmorda clicked her tongue and shook her head. "You are a pale imitation of me. Just look what you've done to yourself. You've let yourself grow . . . .old and ugly."

"There's beauty in age."

"Don't talk stupid. There's no beauty in wrinkles. Women lose their power when they grow older. They lose the ability to attract men. I won't be invisible. Age diminishes us. Look."

She snapped her fingers, her skin shriveling, her body twisting into an old hag. Warts erupted on her nose, and her face became wizened like a rotten apple. She wore a black, round gown down to her ankles, the material ragged and dusty. She looked like a textbook version of a wicked witch. She approached the men still hanging in midair, against the wall. "Watch," she said to Dolly. "Do you think I'm pretty now?" she asked in a coy voice, then leaned forward for a kiss. Both Clay and Jacob recoiled from the odor of the grave surrounding her.

"See, they want no part of me."

"You are wrong, Mother. It's your evilness that repels them. I have learned

much, living among them these many years. I
invited age. It brought deep friendships, love,
and respect that lasted a lifetime." She went to
the sleeping baby and took Claire's plump
hand in her aged one. "Look at this. See how
we complement each other. Look at the grace
that comes from maturity, the elegance of a
lifetime of experience. Growing old is not
about age, it's learning how to look at life and
love with an eye for the difference between
right and wrong. Recognizing that experience
has taught me not to be impulsive but
patient—trusting the universe and its infinite
wisdom. I have learned that beauty is not
about what's on the outside, but what lies in
the soul."

"Blah, blah, blah. Next, you'll tell me
that you've grown old gracefully." Bavmorda
laughed then, a harsh grating sound.

"No woman should measure her
worth by her looks. Even you have more to
offer than that."

Bavmorda slapped her then. Dolly
rocked on her heels, her face becoming set
and angry. Clay watched Dolly's brows lower
into a single line, her jaw hardening.

"I can do everything you can do. I
don't hurt and maim. Does that negate my
powers?"

"If you don't use them, they're not
powers," Bavmorda said.

Dolly balled her fists and shook them. "I'm a better witch than you!" She flung herself at Bavmorda. The older witch evaded her.

"Trout!" Bavmorda called. "Where is that idiot? Never around when you need him."

They collided in the center of the room. The air crackled. Clay watched helplessly as they punched and kicked, Dolly's face growing red with the effort. She charged, her hands outstretched. Sparks flew from their fingers, small colorful balls of lightning whizzing around the room. Dolly tossed one at her mother's face. It glanced off Bavmorda's cheek, leaving a scorch mark, then landed on the floor near the drapes. A breeze blew into the room, ruffling the material. Sparks caught and flames licked at the curtains.

"Claire!" Clay shouted.

Bavmorda cackled with glee. She ran along the walls, perpendicular to the room. Dolly took off after her, using the chandelier to swing to the opposite wall.

The room filled with smoke. Clay and Jacob struggled against the invisible bonds holding them. The fire sizzled, and the room grew hot. The witches fought on, oblivious to the inferno.

Clay heard screams behind them. Lydia stood in the opening, her hand over her mouth.

"Get out, Lydie!" Jacob screamed.

She looked at the fire and ran in the other direction. Clay yelled, tears streaming down his face. "No, come back. Take the baby!" His body was wracked with coughing.

Moments later, Lydia reappeared, a bucket in her hands. She moved toward the fire, skirting the flying women.

Bavmorda saw the girl and the bucket; she covered her face with fright. Still locked in a fight with Dolly, Bavmorda disengaged herself and started toward the exit in panic. Dolly stepped on her long skirt, imprisoning her. Bavmorda was panting and her face had lost all its color. Sound receded and Clay watched the frisson of fear overwhelm the old witch's expression. He glanced at the girl and the pail she was holding.

Clay called urgently, "No, Lydie. Throw the water on Bavmorda!"

"No!" Bavmorda screamed. She raised her hands to place a spell; Dolly wrapped her arms around her, locking her hands to her sides.

"Do it now!" Dolly yelled to the girl.

The room was filled with smoke; Clay could see the two witches struggling in midair.

"Throw the damn water on her and get the baby out of here!" he called.

Lydie tossed the water, bathing both women in a heavy splash. Bavmorda shrieked, her body reacting as if she was being splashed with acid. Smoke enveloped her, creating steam under her clothing. She screamed as she disintegrated, her voice becoming fainter as she dissolved.

The fire in the room fizzled and went out as if it was smothered.

Clay watched Dolly close her eyes, her skin melting. She took a long, last look at Clay, her eyes pools of sadness. "I'm sorry," she said as her voice faded. She slid to the floor, her body disappearing into the carpet, leaving a pile of empty clothes.

Clay fell from the wall, landing onto the floor with a thump. Jacob dropped next to him. Jacob waved his hands, the dissipating smoke burning his eyes. Clay scrambled to his feet, grabbing the dozing baby in his arms. Claire stretched and smiled as if she'd just awoken from a deep nap. Her delighted face lit up when she saw her father. He hugged her, making her soft cheeks wet with his tears. "Let's get out of here."

Trout ran in, holding his head. "Man, I musta' drank too much. You wouldn't believe what . . . hey, Sheriff Finnes." He looked around the mess in the room. "I didn't do nuthin' wrong, so don't start on me. You seen my cousin, Bobby Ray? I can't find him."

BULWARK

Clay pushed past him and took his child home.

16

ONE WAY TO END A STORY
(ENDING 1)

Clay herded the survivors outside. The house buzzed with new energy, which filled him as well. Claire rested her head on his shoulder as if they'd never been parted. He kept kissing her forehead, her tiny hand clutching the material of his shirt.

They congregated in a group outside the old Victorian. "Look!" Lydia pointed to the mansion. It shimmered at first; then the air grew thick, as if it were a gel. The colors of the shutters ran and the clapboards became distorted, as if the entire house was melting on the outside.

They saw a squad car pull up. Terence and Sherri hopped out. "Clay!" Sherri yelled. "What happened here? Is that Claire?"

Clay nodded with a happy smile. He glanced at Terence, who grinned as if they'd never fought. He saluted him, and Clay asked, "Are you okay, Terence? Back to normal?"

"Yeah, sorry. Food poisoning." Terence shrugged sheepishly, patting his stomach.

"Yeah, right, if that's what you want to call it."

Sherri looked at him to the baby. "Care to explain?"

Clay shook his head. "I don't think I can process it. Talk to the kid, Jacob." He jerked his head in the boy's direction. "He'll give you a statement. I have to get home. Get these people to the hospital." He hopped in his car.

"Wait, Clay, you need a car seat for her." Sherri followed him.

Clay shook his head. "I'll hold her. I'm never letting go of her again."

Clay drove slowly, cradling his daughter. She sat in his lap, secure and safe, his strong arms creating a haven.

He pulled into Jenna's development, seeing his wife waiting at her front door as if she knew he'd be coming. She screamed with joy, leaping down the stoop, running to Clay. The impact would have sent another man reeling, but he was her bulwark and could stand her onslaught. Clay hugged his family close, knowing he'd never be alone again.

Later, after Claire fell asleep between them on the bed, Clay lay with his newly bandaged arm resting protectively on his daughter's body. Jenna caressed his shoulder, her eyes soft. They created a protective wall around their child, their heads meeting intimately on the pillows. She stroked his hair.

"There was nothing between Dayna and me. Never was. Do you believe me?" he told her.

Jenna nodded. "I know that. I think I always knew that. It's just that when I had the breakdown, I figured you didn't want me anymore."

Clay wiped a tear that ran down her cheek. "It's always been about 'in sickness and in health.' Nothing else ever mattered to me. I only want you. I always have."

Jenna looked down, her fingers tracing the lines of his collarbone. Clay held his breath, his mind on the aftershave and razor in the medicine closet.

Much as he wanted to let it go, he was afraid to ask if Kent meant something to her.

Her big blue eyes looked up at him. Uh oh, here it comes, he thought with dread.

Jenna looked at him sheepishly. "I'm sorry I threw the badge. It's just that, Dayna—" Jenna began again after a long swallow. "—she's everything a man wants. Beauty, brains, a great . . . ."

Clay shook his head and placed a finger over her lips. Simply touching her sent a thrill up his arm that moved through his chest to reach his heart. He shivered. "Stop. Dayna who? Not interested. Never was and never will be. She's not my type."

Jenna looked at him sheepishly. "I'm sorry I threw the badge."

Clay shrugged as if it didn't matter. It didn't.

"What is your type, anyway?" Jenna asked him, her eyes meeting his.

Clay didn't answer. He leaned over and kissed his wife. "Jenna?"

"Hmm," she responded, her eyes closed; she kissed him again.

Her hand found him, and she slid her fingers under his belt. Clay made a noise and Jenna's eyes flew open. "Quiet, you'll wake Claire." She smiled dreamily and began the assault on his body again.

"I just want to know . . ." He said between kisses.

Jenna sucked on his lower lip, making it hard for him to think.

"Jenna, I . . . understand we weren't together. The aftershave in the bath . . ."

Jenna stopped feathering kisses on his chest. "What?" Jenna looked up puzzled.

"When I slept here the other night. I found a razor and aftershave in your bathroom."

She kissed him on the lips again, her mouth soft and pliant. He groaned with desire, and she laughed. "Shhh, you'll wake her. Some people don't know how to be quiet." Clay's heart plummeted. "Was it serious?" he asked, his voice hoarse.

"Very. I had everything for him here. Let me show you." She rolled off the bed.

Clay felt bereft. He should have never asked. "Was it Peter Kent?" Clay asked, trying hard to prepare himself for the answer.

"Peter?" Jenna laughed out loud then covered her mouth. "He's such a troll! Ugh." Jenna opened the closet door. Three men's shirts hung, a pair of jeans, his boots.

His boots?

"I've been waiting for you to come home. It's all new except for your boots. I had them with me the whole time in the hope we'd stop this foolishness. This is where you belong."

Clay took her in his arms, and they sank to the floor.

It seemed, he discovered, that he could be quiet after all.

17

OR MAYBE YOU'D PREFER AN ALTERNATE ENDING (NUMBER 2)

A persistent beep penetrated Clay's skull, winding its way to the center, where it promised to split his head in half.

He was hot. He shifted on the damp sheets, only to have pain shoot from his hip to his toe. Exquisite and white-hot, it throbbed with wicked intensity. He must have blacked out for a moment because when he opened his eyes, he saw Jenna's eager face leaning over him. Her hand rested on his bandaged ribs.

"Clay, Clay, can you hear me?"

Gritting his teeth, he forced his lids to rise. Jenna looked terrible. Her blonde hair was greasy, as if she hadn't washed it in a week. Her eyes looked swollen, dark circles underneath. She was too thin. He opened his mouth to tell her but found the effort of talking too hard.

He wet his dry mouth, and she placed a spoonful of ice chips on his lips. He lapped them up. "Did they all make it out of the house?"

"House? What house."

He swallowed, his throat hurt to talk. "What's wrong with my throat?"

"They intubated you. It was touch and go . . . never mind. You're going to be fine. Peter said . . ."

"Dr. Kent?" Clay attempted to rise.

"Clay! Stop. You'll break the stitches." She rested her body against him, preventing him from moving.

His eyes opened wide. "Claire! Is she okay?"

"Claire is home. Snug as a bug, waiting for her daddy to recover."

Clay lifted his head and looked around the room. It was filled with monitors. His arm was bandaged. An orderly came in, their eyes locking. Clay stiffened.

"Trout, not now. Come back when he's more himself." Jenna took her phone and started texting messages. "Everybody is going to be so happy. It was a bad accident."

"Accident?"

Jenna brushed the hair back from his face. "You're still warm. Yes, accident. Some couple from Atlanta. It was a head-on collision. . . . Do you remember any of it?"

"Owen's dead," Clay said.

"Oh, you're remembering . . . yes . . . he died on impact. Don't get upset." She adjusted his meds, and he felt the world go soft.

"You and Peter," he mumbled. "The witch was . . . "

"There's no witch." She leaned closer. "Stop saying that, and there's no me and Peter, either." She giggled. "There's a Terence and Peter, though."

Clay's eyes closed. He dozed lightly, knowing Jenna was there, holding his hand. He felt her tickle his cheek. "She's here," she said in a soft voice near his ear. "Claire wants to see her daddy. I found a new sitter. She's been wonderful. Claire adores her," Jenna prattled on as he drifted.

Clay roused. His daughter was on the other side of the glass, waving to him happily.

He smiled, but his eyes widened when he realized who was holding his child. An old woman held her. She was a tiny, shriveled thing, like a . . .

Clay pushed himself up, terror making his heart race. Bavmorda stood holding Claire, a smile on her face that never reached her eyes. They stared at him like the twin bores of a rifle. She raised a hand and waved, nodded once, letting him know that sometimes both dreams and reality could be a nightmare.

AUTHOR'S NOTE

I started Bulwark as part of an anthology that somehow never developed, but I loved the characters too much not to publish it. This was my first attempt at writing adult fiction, and I must say, I am hooked.

Of course, Bulwark does not exist in Georgia. Every character is fictitious.

I was kicking around the idea of doing another book about this special town when R. L. Jackson came up with the idea of using it in a new anthology.

How exciting! Just the idea of seeing these characters live on through the imaginations of other artists is a thrilling idea.

I am looking forward to reading and sharing the upcoming sequels to this story and hope you, dear reader, have as much fun with it as I have.

Special thanks to my assistant, Brittney Leigh Bass, for her commitment and diligence to this project.

For more on my books or to get in touch with me–

Visit my website-
britlunden.com

Like my Facebook page-
facebook.com/britlunden

Follow me on Twitter-
twitter.com/BritLunden

Huge thanks to cover designer R.L. Jackson
authorrljackson.com

Read on for the first chapter from The Missing Branch, Volume Five of The Bulwark Anthology

The Knowing

Brit Lunden

1

JB closed the door gently, glad to have the place to himself again. Sheriff Clay Finnes had taken the injured couple to the hospital.

The only sound in the cabin was the creak of the wooden floors settling and the tick of the antique regulator clock that hung on the wall.

THE KNOWING

It was an old clock and had never worked very well. JB smiled, thinking Ellie would be pleased to see the ornate second hand traveling around the parchment-colored face and the great brass pendulum swinging again.

It must have been set off when he slammed the door shut after he had escorted that ungrateful wretch out of his house. *What a creep, calling his wife a witch, of all things. Didn't she know not to speak ill of the dead?*

He recalled that there was a key lying around somewhere. His wife used to wind that clock every so often and then stand next to it pleading hopefully, "Tick, pretty please!"

The old mechanism would give a muffled gong, move a minute or two, and then stall, making his diminutive wife steam up like a teapot.

It was her great-great-grandmother's, the only piece of her family history willed to her. The rest went to her brother, who married a Northerner and didn't disappoint the family.

That old clock was made by none other than George Mitchell of Bristol, Connecticut, at the beginning of the nineteenth century.

JB concentrated on the etching painted on the reverse glass of the case. It was a pastoral scene, with women holding parasols and men wearing pantaloons and beaver top hats. He noticed the mahogany case was layered with a coating of dust. He ran a crooked finger down the top, leaving a trail. *It's been neglected*, he thought and shook his head. His right knee twinged, and he chuckled, *like me*.

JB had seen many clocks like this one in his day. Despite its Yankee past, every family around here worth their salt had a similar one in their home, to be handed down through the ages.

Every family except his, perhaps.

His family had left him nothing.

JB grabbed a rag on the way to the living room, wiping the water rings from the surface of the coffee table. He'd given the victims of the car accident coasters, but they had carelessly placed them on the surface of the furniture. He'd made that piece for his wife from a tree felled by Hurricane Agnes in '72.

That tree had nearly killed them all, landing on the back of the cottage and taking out the kitchen and half of the dining room with it. JB had gotten his wife and kids out just in time, hiding in the underground root cellar until the worst of the storm had passed.

His eyes smarted now, and he swiped them with a gnarled hand, his loud sniff filling the silence.

He glanced up, blinking several times to clear his eyes, and focused on the picture of Ellie. He picked it up, his hand caressing the face, wishing he could feel her skin.

How dare she? he thought again, bitterly. *How dare that woman say his beloved was a witch?*

Ellie Straton was the sweetest woman to grace the earth, and JB missed her with every fiber of his being.

JB shut his eyes, too tired to think. His mind kept replaying the earlier part of the day over and over again.

He wanted to go back in time and ignore the sound of the blaring horn.

He could still recall the commotion outside that had interrupted his late-afternoon news program.

Grabbing a shotgun, he had thrown on an old sweater and navigated the rickety steps out of the cottage. He had struggled down the path leading to the main road, gripping his gun tightly.

A cold snap in the weather had made his old injury act up, slowing his movements and leaving him sleepless at night. Still, he had hefted the gun close since one couldn't be too careful. He had paused for a minute to give the clearing by the woods a good look. It was only yesterday he had seen a wolf lurking in a thicket at the end of his property.

He'd have to remember to tell the sheriff about it.

JB was sure that wolves were extinct in this part of Georgia.

At first, he had reckoned it might be a stray. He knew Bobby Ray and Trout Parker kept a pack of mongrels that annoyed most of the local farmers. Those mutts were known to raid the chicken houses, wreaking havoc on the best layers in the county.

He thought about the animal he had seen yesterday. *It could have been a dog.* He felt himself wavering. *No it was definitely a wolf.* He shook his head. *It was one big, bad-looking wolf.*

Frankly, he wasn't used to seeing much of anything on this side of town.

Most people stayed on the other end of Bulwark, especially since that smelly, green puddle had appeared out of nowhere.

He had reported stagnant water as soon as he had noticed it about ten days ago, but nobody cared.

THE KNOWING

It was on the Old Jericho Road that folks didn't travel anymore. Everyone knew the street had fallen out of use when the mill shut down years ago.

JB shook his craggy head. *People had no business traveling in that direction.* Strange stories had always come from that end of the county, even before he was born.

Some claimed spirits walked the woods and meadows; others said evil lurked there. Either way, from the time he was knee-high and the size of a tree stump, he knew to stay away.

Even talking about it gave him the willies, and that took a lot.

There was very little that frightened JB Straton, but for as long as he could remember, going into that neck of the woods was considered forbidden. Not that he believed in mumbo-jumbo. But somehow he had always taken those warnings seriously. *Damn, if he couldn't explain it, nobody could.*

JB Straton considered himself a rational man most of the time. However, there were those instances that gave him pause, especially with Ellie.

JB surveyed the growing pond filling the roadway, the shrill blast of the car horn making his heart beat a little faster in his chest. That sound could only mean someone was in trouble.

JB had looked for a source of the spreading water but didn't see where it started.

He knew the puddle was far from the creek that ran parallel to the back of his home. It was apparent it wasn't coming from there. Besides, that water was pure and clean, and this looked like sewage to him.

Only last week it had started as a puddle, and today, it looked like it had grown into a small pond, he grumbled. The smell was intolerable, the greenish color made it look like industrial waste.

Clay Finnes should have come earlier and investigated, he said to himself at the time.

He liked Clay well enough, had even voted for him. But maybe taking on the top job as sheriff was too much for the man. JB knew Clay was understaffed from budget cuts, and of course, there was that business about his child and his disintegrating marriage. *Sad stuff, kidnapping, right here in safe little Bulwark.*

Cries mixed with the discordant sound of the horn had brought him back to himself. JB slid down the embankment, landing in ankle-deep ooze.

He had slipped, catching himself but feeling the tight tendons on his leg protest. Cursing strangers, overgrown puddles, and his own bum knees, he had made his way resentfully toward the water. He had halted at the edge, considering his options.

THE KNOWING

A lone car, a Ford Fusion, was stuck in the middle of the quagmire. *City folk*, he muttered under his breath. Any sensible country person would never attempt to drive through deep water like that unless they had a truck.

A woman calf-deep in the water was trying to pull a man from the driver's side. JB shook his head grimly. The origin of the noise was her companion's head pressed against the steering wheel.

"Hey!" JB had called. "Hey, is everything okay?"

The stranger had looked in his direction, her eyes unfocused. She waved her hands. She was shouting something, but he could barely hear her.

He had squinted at her, turning his better ear in her direction to try to catch what she was saying.

She had screeched about her children and witches.

Witches? He had huffed. *Another nutjob looking for entertainment at the expense of the locals.* Last year, a film crew all the way from Hollywood had camped out on the edge of Sam Holsteam's farm, searching for the ghosts from a Civil War battle said to have occurred there.

The cast and crew had skedaddled quickly enough, screaming bloody murder. Everybody in town knew the film crew had left pasty-faced and hungover from Sam's peach moonshine. *City slickers*, he had snickered, *couldn't handle a good jug of 'shine.*

"Do you need help?" he had shouted to the woman.

This time, when she had looked at him, he had noticed a thin line of blood trickling from her hairline.

JB had patted his back pocket. He had hissed under his breath, calling himself five kinds of fool.

He'd forgotten that blasted cell phone his kid insisted he keep on him at all times in case he fell or something.

JB had bent awkwardly, placing the gun on the dry part of the incline and then gingerly stepping into the slimy puddle. He had realized that he had never changed into boots as his slippers filled with cold water.

Gritting his teeth, he had fought the urge to leave. *Why hadn't he removed the slippers?* Ellie had bought those slippers for him their last Christmas together. Now, they'd be ruined; his jaw twitched with resentment.

JB had waded toward the vehicle as the woman grew increasingly incoherent. As he had moved her out of the way, one of her flailing hands had caught him on the side of his head, and JB swore he heard bells ringing.

"No, stop it, woman. I'm here to help."

He had held her by both her shoulders, trying to reason with her, but she had looked as dazed as Johnny Gottfried had when he collided with a linebacker and suffered the worst concussion the NFL had ever recorded.

Her eyes had rolled in their sockets, and he saw her face drain of what little color it had. He had shaken her gently. "Now, don't go and faint on me, ma'am. I can't carry you both."

This had seemed to reach her, and she had whimpered.

She had grabbed the collar of his sweater, her bloody fingers poking holes in the fragile weave.

"My children . . . my children. Wicked, wicked place." She had looked like a wild woman, her mouth stretched in a soundless scream.

She had snagged a thread on his sweater when she grabbed him, loosening it. JB had watched it unravel and fought the urge to brush her away. *Ellie had knitted this sweater. How much more was this day going to cost him?*

JB had taken a steadying breath and then patiently turned the woman in the direction of his house. He had given her a poke to the center of her back. "Go there." He had pointed up the embankment. "I'll get your husband out."

He had watched her slog through the water to the other side, her head lowered.

Satisfied she was making progress, he had turned back to the man. His head rested against the steering wheel, his eyes were closed, and his skin had a faint bluish cast.

"Mister?" JB had called over the noise of the horn. He had touched the skin of the man's neck, recoiling at the clammy feel. This was not looking very good.

JB had wavered with the idea of moving him. He realized the water was now inching up over JB's thighs.

Again, he had looked for the source of the water, but had seen nothing except a widening greenish body of muck.

The door to the car was open and rapidly flooding with water. JB reached in, and using his upper body strength attempted to move the man. He couldn't budge him. JB placed his shoulder under the victim's arm and half dragged the man from the vehicle. He had been rewarded with a low groan, but the victim had definitely been nothing more than dead weight.

He had managed to get the couple into his cottage, wrap them both in blankets, and call the sheriff.

Tea with brandy had revived the wife enough for her to notice her surroundings.

It was then that she had focused on his Ellie's picture on the mantle and had accused his wife of stealing her children. Sheriff Clay Finnes had arrived just then, as his patience was wearing thin, along with that pushy news reporter Dayna Dalton. The injured couple was taken away, and he was left to the thick silence that felt like a comforting old blanket.

He was well rid of the intruders and now looked around his peaceful home, wishing his unwanted guests a speedy recovery along with the hope that he never had to set eyes on them again.

JB shuffled over to his recliner, his worn knees protesting.

He had changed his clothes after the whole hullabaloo but still felt chilled to the bone. *Took a long time to warm this old body*, he remembered ruefully.

He rubbed the skin of his thigh, the site of another football injury so horrible the bone had snapped and torn through his skin. *What was it, forty-four or forty-five years ago?*

He remembered waking from surgery, Ellie's hand brushing his forehead, her soft voice assuring him his football career had not ended.

He cleared his throat noisily, tears smarting his eyes, happy that Ellie wasn't here to witness it. *How dare that woman accuse his wife of being a witch? Not his Ellie, his soul mate, his life.*

JB settled into his chair, pulling the hand-knitted afghan over his knees. His head rolled, and with it, his memories unspooled like an old-time movie.

Read the rest of the Bulwark Anthology!

Bulwark by Brit Lunden

The Knowing, Volume 1 by Brit Lunden

The Illusion, Volume 2 by DJ Cooper

The Craving, Volume 3 by R.L. Jackson

The Window, Volume 4 by E.H. Graham

The Missing Branch, Volume 5 by Kay MacLeod

The Body, Volume 6 by Kate Kelley

The Battle of Bulwark, Volume 7 by Del Henderson III

The Darkness, Volume 8 by Brittney Leigh

If you enjoyed this story, please leave a review on Amazon, Goodreads, or wherever else you love to talk about books. Thank you!

CPSIA information can be obtained
at www.ICGtesting.com
Printed in the USA
FFHW010732311019
55888904-61760FF